HorrorCon

Scott Norton

yellow horse

First Published in the United States of America in 2008
by Yellow Horse Publishing

ISBN 978-0-6152-3900-2

Yellow Horse Publishing
LANDISVILLE, NJ 08326-0227

Contents

Friday

Saturday

Friday

part one

Eliza Lowell was a gypsy. Well, her ancestors were. That's what she chose to believe, anyway, once she discovered that her last name was connected to someplace in Romania. The fact that she was the daughter of an Irish woman and a man who carried the name of his adoptive parents didn't matter. She could feel her roots, and today she was going to need them if she was going to pick up her act and get to the convention.

Her "authentic monster artifacts" auction company, Once Bidden, was doing well. "Well" as in "barely breaking even", but still well enough for her to afford to make another trip to another hotel where she would be among her people again; the people who loved – scratch that – *lived* for horror and everything associated with it. Films, novels, graphic novels, plastic figurines, fashions of the dark; it was all there, stacked high to the ceiling and for as far as the eye could see. And despite what her father thought about what the attendees and dealers wore or how they dyed and cut their hair, she knew they were among the kindest and gentlest souls that she had ever encountered. Sure, lots of assholes loved to take in a gore flick on the way to punching and kicking the life out of an innocent boy before turning on his girlfriend as she fought them off hoping for someone to help, to care, to just look their way and lay on a car horn. But those types were scum, which in truth was an insult to scummy things everywhere.

She didn't want to think about all that right now. She couldn't.

If she did, she would throw her homemade banner full of fanged fonts and demon graphics and all of her authentic, monster relics back down into the garage below her $150 a week dump of an apartment. Then, she would crawl back into her pitch-black tomb of a bedroom until the sun went down and the day didn't look so painful. Speaking of pain, her neck was hurting again. She would have to take some more painkillers if she even wanted to entertain the idea of making it to the hotel and setting up her booth. She just hoped that this time she would guess correctly as to exactly how many would draw the heat from her nerve endings, but not the alertness from her mind. Three pills should do it. Yeah, three sounded right. She never took less than three.

She took them down with a quick gulp from the rest of that morning's Red Bull and threw her black, Frankenbunny hoodie over her head. Six months ago she would have spent another hour making sure her hot-Goth look was perfect. The thigh-high vinyl boots, the second-skin leggings, the studded choker, the tight-as-her-food-budget tank dress – all would be applied with a seductive artist's touch. But six months ago she didn't need pain pills. Six months ago she had a boyfriend to impress as well as scores of convention regulars who loved to debate with her about whether the contents of the tiny bags of hair she sold actually came from a real Yeti, or if the claws she had strung together to make a necklace were really from France and had once actually belonged to a gargoyle. No, six months after the day the blurry-faced filth stomped her sweet Ryan to death and violently violated her before leaving her for the vultures, she had no interest in how she looked beyond checking to see if that last bit of swelling had gone down. It's a sad fact of convention life that everyone likes to stop at the sob story table, but hardly anyone wants to buy from it. No, she needed money for doctors and makeup – lots of makeup – and today was all about business.

She hadn't talked to her fellow "Children of the Fright" in weeks. Sure, they had been there for her after, and stopped by with movies and incense and stuff, but then it had gotten much too hard to see them. The comfort of their touch, their caressing fingers, all turned to hot, burning reminders of how he used to feel. Jesse, Ryan's best friend, was about his height and soft in the same places. He lacked the broadness of Ryan's shoulders but they were so close and so much alike they practically wore the same thing everyday and cut their hair exactly the same way. She always loved Ryan's hair. It was longish and stood up stupidly the second the wind touched it. And his eyes were the kindest eyes she had ever seen. There were times when they would show a hint of rage or a glint of delicious fear, but she could always see the goofy boy that lived behind them. Even when he painted heavy liner around the outside to piss off the homophobic skinheads downtown, those eyes always gave away what he really was: the sweetest, most creative soul she had ever met. Jesse might have been a close second, but to touch him now caused her the kind of pain they don't make pills for – unless you're talking about the kind that have no recommended dosage because the entire bottle was the only thing that did the trick.

She felt the worst about Lily. She and Lily had known each other since they were four years old. Both hadn't really had any friends before they met, and never really had any after – not the *thisclose* kind, anyway. They shared the same thoughts, loves, likes, tastes and clothes just like Ryan and Jesse. It was a perfect foursome, but like most perfect things, the smallest change can often bring the whole thing down. They didn't know how good they had it being together, and how impossible it would be to regain that once one of them was gone. It was as if they had created new identities through each other's chemistry and took for granted that these super-inhuman personas would last outside the existence of their close-knit cube of non-conformity. Lily had given everything to convince her that they could be who they were again. She had sent notes, written stories and songs, and was pretty handy with Adobe Photoshop putting them all back together again for some other time, some other place. But this was now and here, and the pain was kicking her ass every second she tried to ignore it and move on. Those days were over, at least for now, and like a look down angry Samara's well in *The Ring*, the end was nowhere in sight.

But today it was time to try, if only for the money. Her inventory was starting to smell, and some of it was looking kind of squished. Most of it she had gotten off of eBay, but a small portion of her treasure she had found scouring the farthest corners of the internet. It was easy, really. Sites like Babelfish made it possible for you to read the funny writing of foreign languages, and once you got in the habit of using it, the world literally opened up in exponential dimensions. One website in the Netherlands linked to another in Peru, and that one linked to yet another somewhere in New Zealand or Bangladesh. There were people out there who believed – just like she used to believe – that The Boogeyman was real and they had the evidence to prove it. It's funny in a not-so-funny kind of way: when things are going well, it's easy to think that there could be such a thing as a flying creature with the face of a man and the teeth and appetite of a crocodile, but when life finally got its bloody hooks in you, all of that suddenly seemed completely ridiculous. That would be the hardest part: looking those who stopped by the table in the eye and giving them the story with a straight face. She would just have to try and focus on the money in their pockets and tell herself that the con was worth it. And hell, if they believed it, who was she to take that away from them just because she was no longer living the dream? Just because the veil had been lifted from her reality, that didn't mean she had to poke holes in anyone else's perfectly functioning shroud. And while these thoughts made her feel ashamed, somewhere deep inside where she used to feel safe – where she kept the memories of Ryan and their fearsome foursome – it also made her feel like a survivor. It hadn't been so long since she had felt incapable of taking another breath that she could afford to refuse these little lies. And who knows? It just might be that lies would be all she would ever have from now on.

Eliza Lowell was in luck. Above her purple and black Neon traveling just shy of 60 miles per, the Floridian sky was overcast and the temperature was cool even for October. When you're wearing all black – when *all* you wear is black – these sorts of days are blissfully welcome. She had never been one to sully her smooth, pale skin with a beach bitch tan and she didn't want to start today. It sometimes took ten trips to the trunk of her car to get everything into the hotel and that was about all her half-Irish complexion could stand. She was thankful that she was considered pretty even without makeup and the "evil dominatrix" get-up, and even she had to admit to a few good angles in just the right amount of candlelight. Her hair was naturally very dark and still healthy enough to keep as long as she wanted it, which lately was just past her small – and she could swear – shrinking boobs. She had always loved the way her hair made her feel safely hidden from the "non-believers". With a little help from her nose ring, chin-piercing and almost fully sleeved left arm, her hair did the talking for her, sent the signals, and created that all-important "repel zone" that kept the Barbies and Kens at bay.

Before her mother had died and her father and his second family moved away, she had a step-sister that was everything she was not: popular in high school, co-captain of the cheerleading squad, a serial, teen-pageant finalist, and a total Einstein when it came to social gatherings. She was a perfect subject for honing "the look". If Madison looked her up and down and made a face that was one part fear and two parts revulsion, Eliza knew she had pulled it off. Maddie wasn't a mean person, really, just an extremely shallow one. She may have even liked Ryan had she and her stepmom decided that Sarasota was a place worthy of a proper manicure. As it was, they moved up north: Connecticut, maybe. Last anyone heard they were spending the summers there and the winters in Palm Beach. Neither would have had any use for a day like today. Eliza had to giggle a little remembering how the last time she'd seen them, her half-sister had given her this great big cheerleader hug and called her Elisha. Whatever.

The hotel was just where she had left it last July. It looked the same: same dull, grey awning, same tinted rectangular windows, and the same knee-high, square shrubs lined up over the same dried out, decorative mulch. How many cigarettes were still scattered underneath the prickly cover she didn't know, but there must have been thousands. Horror folks smoke. They smoke a lot. In fact, smoking is pretty much the only thing they like to do more than partake in all things horror, and that includes drinking. See, lots of horror folks are on strong medication and can't drink. You can always tell the ones who are, because they're generally the ones who forget to pay for stuff. They don't mean to be rude; they just don't half know where they are.

A horror convention, she thought, is like Christmas for the bad kids. And by "bad", she really meant "misunderstood". She knew how they felt. She always maintained that some horror folks are born, some are made and some are both. She was both. In the beginning it was about the thrill of the unknown, and the sexy lure of the prohibited. She had found a kind of macabre logic in the lurid, leaden horror world that didn't seem to be acknowledged in the lighter corridors of life. The monsters were what they were, and only tried to be something else if that was part of what they were. Deception could be a web to trap prey or to breed, and in a way that was acceptable as long as it was done in horrifyingly spectacular fashion. To a bloodthirsty demon trying to get by, it's mostly about survival in an otherwise hostile world, with a proud touch of demented peacock thrown in.

When Eliza was very young, everyday felt like the first day of school, or going to the doctor's office. Inside, she always felt wrongly institutionalized by every custom and social convention. Growing up, she learned to hide in plain sight before the defiance within burst like a clogged black artery, showing her ruffled, raven feathers and discovering for her the elation of full-blown alienation. After that, she'd never again be the slightest bit interested in running from the dark side of daily existence. Seriously, there could be no sense made of getting your period one-day, and wanting to wear something in a florid pastel the next. Surely, if it was normal to just start bleeding on the swing set at recess, we were all meant to be a little scary. Above all, we were meant to be what we were and damn to hell what anyone else thought about it.

Then, as she grew older, she learned of the world's insistence to throw light onto every shadow in order for the "sheeple", as she called them, to feel closer to some brand of manufactured innocence and purity. There were things you could buy to hide what you were and cover up those desires to run wild into the night and howl at the moon, but none of them felt healthy to her. She was afraid if she didn't accept her need to bare her fangs she would begin to disappear into some kind of exclusionary ether where the only thing one could do to remain on the cloud was push others off. And even today, she hated herself for having to cover up her scars. She loathed her longing for the fuzzy perspective of the world that kept her head high, and her eyes forward. Today wasn't about allegory and imagination; it was about a real darkness not so mysteriously beautiful and titillating but hateful and bland, dishonest and homogenous. It was about everything that the horror she loved was not and yet here she was heading into a throng of believers armed with nothing but sub-minor celebrity. She sure didn't feel like a celebrity right now. Right now every airborne molecule, every last free radical ping-ponging about the lobby ceiling fans, felt like molten liquid hell soaking through her too thin, translucent skin.

Being early Friday afternoon, the twenty-two-story Wyndorf Hotel hadn't yet switched front desk operators for the 5 p.m. kick-off to the convention and the elevators were already dinging a constant one-note melody. However, there was nothing one-note about the variety of dealers that, like Eliza, were shuttling their wares in and out of the East Wing Ballroom. They were all here: the t-shirt guys, the figurine guys, the authentic vintage one-sheet guys, the fledgling low-budget film company guys, the local spook TV variety show guys, and even the tattoo guys who got kicked out last year because they were inking people who were clearly too drunk to come to the conclusion that a permanent vampire bite on their neck was a good idea. With her hoodie up and her hair tucked in, Eliza managed to drift past several faces she recognized without them recognizing her in return. She was a ghost: one that, luckily or not, was still alive and wanting the pills she had swallowed to get the fuck on with it.

"Is the heat on?" she wondered aloud. It took an instant to realize she knew better, and that it was just her nerves. Her anonymity was only going to last so long, which meant she had two choices: ride it out for as long as she could, growing more and more anxious about when her cover would be blown, or test her mettle while everyone was still busy setting things up and announce her arrival. She never had the chance to choose.

"Lies and Love All!"

From the middle of the ballroom came a voice she would always think of whenever she imagined her family dog from childhood, Rufus, who would lay shivering under her bed covers after a round of ghost teasing in the cemetery down the street. They would find a name on a tombstone, the sillier the better, and she and Rufus would make up songs about it. Well, she would sing, and Rufus would pretty much bark at anything she pointed at. When they felt they had done enough damage to the self-esteem of the dearly departed, they would haul ass back to her room and hide from the pissed-off spirits they were certain were chasing them. Under her comforter, Rufus would adopt her panic, the loyal follower that he was, reminding her that it was all just a game and that no one's tortured soul was squeezing through the holes in the window screen. But if Rufus had found his way back to earth after getting hit by that horrible, beige Ford Explorer, he would have done it by possessing the soul of Francis Zeffirelli; the second greatest follower in horror world history.

Francis loved Eliza, or so he believed. It was really just lust repackaged into corny epithets spilled over a rapidly warming Coors Light, rather than a genuine, "'til death do us part" kind of love. He sold lame DVD copies of 70's Eurohorror complete with tacky homemade covers full of as many freeze-frame printouts of boobies he could find. "Sex sells!" he would say, as if everyone in the world over the age of nine hadn't already heard it a hundred times before. The thing was, you got what you saw with Francis. Yes, he was annoying, and yes she could picture him beating off to her in his room when he said he had "gone up for something he forgot". But the truth is he was a crowd favorite for good reason. He would drop the very box he was holding to help set up someone's booth, even if it meant damaging half his inventory and never getting around to finishing his own table. For the past five years she had refused his offer, not wanting to lead him on in even the smallest way. But this year her hip, still not right after being contorted in ways a normal hip was never meant to be contorted, was urging her like a persistent, snake-oil salesman to "try something new".

"Hey," grumbled Eliza. She forced it out like she had finally taken her turn at the receiving line of a wake. She hadn't gotten any practice talking like a social human being for what seemed like weeks and it only just dawned on her that she would have to interact with actual conversation outside of the ready-made spiel she had memorized for customers. But good old Francis, he would wait for an hour, drooling down the front of his extra large *El Topo* t-shirt if it meant that he had her attention – just like good old Rufus.

"What's with the Grim Reaper get-up?" he asked, half like a game show host and half like a twelve year-old still skipping through life blissfully unaware that adults conducted real lives with real problems when they weren't around, and didn't just warehouse themselves in a closet until the next time they saw them.

"I'm cold." It was all she had.

"Yeah, I guess it is kinda cold for Orlando. Supposed to heat up later though, so my advice to you would be to…you know…get into your diva garb."

"If I have time."

"You want me to get your stuff?" he asked, eagerly. "Purple and grey Neon, right?"

At that painfully pubescent moment the pills kicked in. For some reason, it had taken the entire two-hour drive up from Sarasota for this to happen. But as always, once they hit the wait was worth it. There is nothing sweeter than when your stomach hits the switch and with a warm, damp rag wipes the sweaty scowl from your face, leaving you with a cooled layer of fresh skin. It was the second time she had gotten lucky and she hadn't even been there for five minutes. Maybe it was the euphoric wave, the sudden absence of hip pain, or the positive portent that made her nod her head enthusiastically at the man who would be masturbating to a sexed-up mental image of the Grim Reaper in the time it took to rewind a DVD, but whatever it was, she was listening.

"Give me two minutes," he added breathlessly.

You got 'em, sport.

Lies and Love All is what everyone called her who knew her for the last four years she had been coming to Orlando for the convention. It was a slang-abbreviated version of her name, using the Eastern European pronunciation of the "w" in Lowell. So *Eliza Luv-uhl* became *Lies and Love All.* It was what she was selling, they would say. "You buying?" she would retort in her best Miami Beach prostitute. And quicker than you could say "Candyman" five times in the mirror, every available space in front of her $325 rental table would be three deep and panting.

At first, the vaguely Vampirella-like persona she had developed worried her. She didn't want to have to bring that vibe every time and the merchandise she was selling wasn't living flesh. After a few hours, she sniffed something different than pawing "pervs" in a creepy peep show. It was something closer to geek worship than fetish awakening, and she learned fairly quickly that the second you stopped being a cool chick that could hold your own about this movie or that masked psycho you lost them forever. Many a looker had come and gone who figured she would have them eating out of her bustier just for bothering to show up at their little wankfest. The trick was to win their respect by genuinely sharing their interests. You had to walk the walk, sister. Pimple-faced Dan in the Pumpkinhead costume could smell a cheesecake fake from the back of the line and news traveled fast. Real fast.

"Lies!"

And like *that*, the tears ejaculated from Wendy Whipple's eyes and down her cheeks like too-orange blood down Christopher Lee's colorized chin. Wendy was as matronly as Francis was horny, but Eliza wasn't in the mood for either. She sometimes referred to the approaching middle-aged, skull connoisseur as "Whimple"; not to her face of course, because, well, she would cry. When the dealers finally all got a break from pushing product, they'd occasionally bypass the bar and head up to one of the meeting rooms showing a classic horror flick. Most of the time the selections would correspond to the featured guests of the show, like *The Evil Dead* when Bruce Campbell was in town or *The Lost Boys* when Corey Feldman was slumming back east. But no matter what it was, Wendy cried through the whole thing. She cried when the first sex-starved teens died having sex in the back of a convertible in the middle of the woods and she cried when their killer finally zigged when he should have zagged and lost his neck. No one could actually tell if she was sad or happy during these moments. Most just assumed that her pipes were laid wrong and it was as natural to her as whistling through a graveyard. Needless to say, Eliza did not need to see Wendy right now. But like a bejeweled, magenta–headed, generously curved malaise settling over an otherwise tenuously stable situation, there she was, all ready to jack in and jag.

She wrapped her arms around Eliza as if trying to hold her together, and despite the pills kicking in only moments earlier, shooting pains from about seven different places in her body traveled straight to her tear ducts. Great, now they were both crying.

“I’ve been so worried about you,” Wendy sung into her ear, each note drenched with Siouxsie Sioux sympathy.

“I’m fine,” Eliza lied. “Really,” she lied again.

“Those bastards...and the way that asshole defense lawyer got your testimony thrown out on account of a little amnesia...I can’t even think about it or I’ll start to cry.”

“Don’t do that. You’ve got a long day. We both do.” Nothing Eliza said sounded like her saying it. To even consider how long the day was going to be was impossible. It already felt like she had been there for a week’s worth of long days.

“You listen to me,” Wendy instructed, “if there’s anything you need, anything at all, you know where to find me.”

“Yep.” Eliza assured her. “Out in the hall behind a mountain of glass skulls.”

“That’s right”, said Wendy. “Just give me a yell or send Igor the Horror Monkey out to get me and we’ll have you propped up and smiling in no time.”

At that moment, Francis walked back into the ballroom. He had somehow managed to get everything in one trip, even if it did mean risking damaging something banging into the sides of the doorway as he passed through. He knew instantly to whom she was referring.

“Hey! Monkeys are people too, you know,” he objected.

Wendy pulled up the tip of her nose and said, “Except when they’re pigs!”

Wendy had stopped crying long enough to almost make Eliza laugh, so she figured she owed her one.

“You bet,” Eliza said. “Thanks, Wendy.”

Wendy hugged her again, sending another round of fire through her central nervous system.

“You don’t have to thank me,” she said, “you know that.”

Eliza, stifling a scream, had to agree.

By 5:30, the Wyndorf was teeming with horror faithful flooding into every available corner. Still wrapped in her hoodie, she mentally negotiated the onrushing tide by imagining them as black jellybeans being poured into a jetsam jar for subsequent disposal.

And thank gods for all the black. Black made her feel sane, safe, *even-keeled*. To the average guest happening upon the event on their way into the complimentary buffet, it might have seemed like the gates of hell had opened up. She knew some people who never wore black, afraid to be perceived as too edgy and angry, perhaps. But that's not why she wore black, or, she surmised, half of this mob did either. Sure, brightly colored facsimiles to one's horror hero of choice looked best popping off the dark fabric, but a black outfit is more about matching one's internal rhythm than a slimming fashion. Black is a color that is comfortable with pain, but it also encompasses of all the colors in the spectrum. Black "gets it" as a color. It's not on some kind of heady, bullshit, upwardly mobile trip. It's content with resting at the bottom, cause the bottom is where the heavy shit falls. And lots of these folks are carrying the heavy. She sure as hell was. Best to be down where it's expected from the start, than up where one slip sends you tumbling, fingers pointing, eyes averting.

Still, she couldn't stop trembling. She closed her eyes as she pretended to shift around a few items, hoping that the first round of "merch" hounds would behave to type: do a loose lap, have a look, and hold onto their cash and questions until they had mentally maximized their budget over a cocktail. Maybe her skin would stop crawling by the time the first exchange bubbled up to the oily surface. Maybe it would take one to ease her terror. And that was exactly what it was that she was feeling: pure terror.

"Oh wow...intense." The voice sounded soft, male and sleepy. She couldn't look up to respond, but quickly accessed a support group chorus that she didn't even know was there: *"Come on, basket case, it's time to get back on the broom. Breathe, take a look at what he's referring to, and fall into the pitch. They just want to have fun and they're willing to give you money for the honor if you just play along. Just...look...up..."*

When she did he was already at the next table. He looked back but Eliza turned away immediately only to lock eyes with a kind-looking couple fingering a few of the silver knives that supposedly robbed a lycanthrope family in northern Canada of its slower members. The info was right there on an index card that she filled out so long ago, she had forgotten to change the year. It wasn't smart to have merchandise that looked like it had been sitting around for too long as if thousands of others had previously asked, trashed and passed on it and that was exactly what it was.

"Where do you find this stuff?" The woman seemed open enough to let the sad little girl in the hoodie explain before she laughed it off. Six, long, tortuous months ago that would have been all she needed. Today, what she needed, what she *really* needed, was to throw up.

"Excuse me." A quick duck under the table and it was out of the frying pan and into the fucking volcano. Eliza started to cry and immediately felt like shit for teasing Wendy all these years. Francis saw her and Wendy must have clued him in because he was ignoring his customers and tracking her with grave concern. She secretly hoped he would knock a few attendees over so she could get through, but she was moving against a relentless, dark tide and even a bulky horndog like Francis wouldn't have made a dent if he had belly-flopped from the chandelier.

The chandelier. That perfectly boring noun was now helping her fight back the bile that she knew was on its way to the back of her throat. She looked up as she pushed against the lumbering masses and found one of the twinkling monstrosities hovering disapprovingly. She studied it, probably for the first time. Its twinkling glass tears seemed to cry for her as it hung heavy, also wanting to be anywhere else but right there, right then. Without taking her eyes from it she worked her way down the rest of the aisle, turned the corner at a row of t-shirt racks, threaded through a lucky break in the action in front a Giallo double-table display and found herself outside in the harsh light of the lobby hall.

At that point it was all about the pug ugly rug. At any other time, the gaudy pattern would have made her nauseous. But she was already nauseous, and like the chandelier, its hideous incongruence had a reversing effect on her stomach. The stay of purgation was clearly temporary, so she immediately picked up the pace. In exactly twenty-seven steps she'd entered the ladies lavatory, with ten more getting her inside the minor miracle of an available stall. She dropped to her knees as if to give thanks for the pills already having been digested, and inelegantly deposited approximately three sips of warm Red Bull and fuck knows what else into the waiting toilet bowl.

Contents exhausted, Eliza rocked back onto the seat of her too loose-fitting jeans and leaned against the stall wall. She had no idea how she was going to stand up again, let alone return to her table, and all she wanted was to be back in her bed, waiting for sleep. This morning she had found the courage to make it this far. Now, any reserves of strength she had left were spinning around at the bottom of a ceramic bowl. Would she end up spending the rest of the weekend on the floor of the Wyndorf's public bathroom? She hadn't even made it into her room yet, and the prospect of never seeing it seemed far more likely than her getting to her feet. Even if she could get her legs working again, remaining in the six-foot by three-foot stall forever sounded about right for how she felt inside: like total shit.

Friday

part two

Dr. Dimitrji Radan popped the top, middle button on the collar of his shirt and brushed any remaining lint from his suit jacket with measured swipes of each hand. He looked quite young for his age, which was a number he never shared with anyone. Most people put him in his late fifties or early sixties, which suited him just fine.

He had considered wearing a tie due to the unseasonably chilly temperatures, but at the last minute decided against it. He didn't want to be mistaken for hotel staff again. There was only so many times one could direct guests to an ATM machine before it started to feel offensive to one's hard-earned cachet. Yes, he was an author of horror fiction, but one who had also received his doctorate from Bucharest University in anthropological studies, and several years later his PhD in counseling psychology from Yale University. At Yale, he had developed his own hypnotherapy techniques that had earned him several distinguished awards, all of which ended up weighing down this paper or that. Most of his research he had done on himself, but some still considered his methods dangerous. They were "not tested under proper scientific scrutiny, risking potentially dangerous and irreversible side effects", his opponents had roared. However, before the knives were sharpened, he retired. He had more than his share of helping the human race to last several lifetimes.

He had come in early for the convention this time, mostly because the Wednesday overnight flight had been reasonably priced. He also liked to take the extra day on Thursday to acclimate to his new surroundings, and if he felt like it, attend the banquet for invitees that evening. Still, something in the back of his mind told him to get as much out of this one as he could. Ideas were drying up and he no longer could sit at his computer for more than thirty minutes before he felt the need to stretch his legs on the hardwood floor of his study. He was also becoming increasingly uncomfortable with the idea of dredging up the half-memories he needed for the creation of new plots. There were only a few places left to look, and those places had been deemed off-limits. The real problem was that if he couldn't disappear into his novels he was left with very few options. The diagnosis of agoraphobia from a recent fan that also happened to be a certified psychologist made him laugh when people were looking, but in private he knew it wasn't far removed from the truth. Only, he could scarcely remember what the truth was anymore. He was here, had gone to great lengths to make it, and the time spent with his contemporaries last night – even if he had only just poked his head in for a quick brandy which he didn't touch – made him feel warm and welcome for the second time in the span of a year. So they were his choices: sit down and pick his Pandora's lockbox or pace like a madman. Maybe there were enough safe memories gathered in the corners of his mostly vacant reserves to squeeze out another year of free meals, book deals and flattering conversation. The possibility of it, as small as it was, was enough to put a smile on his face and make him pick up his room key. He had always enjoyed the sentiment of hope, even if he had never really been able to feel it since he was a young man.

Seconds before the elevator doors were to open, Dmitrije steeled himself against the inevitable otherness that would ensue upon his emergence. It was a game understood by every honored convention guest between themselves and their fans. They would appear delighted with the demigod worship that would last, without pause, from 5 pm to 8 pm the first night, a neck-breaking stretch from 10 am to 6 pm the following day, and finally, an 11 am to 4 pm final leg if one's constitution hadn't been thoroughly destroyed by then. If all went as planned, the fans would walk away with their prize contemplating how wonderful it must be to be their heroes, and their heroes would contemplate the meaning of it all in the taxi on the way to the airport.

In truth, celebrity brought with it a sliding scale of burdens. It began as a euphoric and welcome validation that marked real achievement, quickly followed by the lamprey attachment of a barely detected psychological addiction. Once financial security was achieved, it soon transformed into an irresistible menace: a state that, when absent created crippling fears of doubt, and when present, crippling bouts of heightened vulnerability. At last, one either developed a mental routine to deal with the alternating neuroses or allowed the teeter-totter to send them down the path of self-destruction. While novelists traditionally garnered a smaller, less rabid following than those in front of the camera, he still insisted on being dispassionately meticulous in his dealing with the degree of fame he had obtained; to the point where he no longer had to think about it save a few seconds between the lower hotel floors. However, in that tiny moment between the elevator coming to rest and the doors yawning apart, he never failed to feel at least a small twinge of apprehension. After all his years on this earth, and everything he had seen, one thing always lay in wait: change. You never knew when it would come, but like the morning sun, it most certainly always did.

Leaving the tie behind turned out to be a subtle stroke of genius. The suit jacket, coupled with his dignified demeanor, was enough to part the sea of memorabilia hounds yet still maintain the all-important air of distinguished guest. Negotiating the lines forming outside the "Celeb Room", which held the dozen or so actors that had made the trip, and into the "Dealers' Room" proved uneventful. He had to click his tongue when he reviewed just how smartly he had managed to straddle the fine line between celebrity guest and celebrated dealer. Actors usually only have their interestingly aged visages and "how they were" publicity photographs to sell, and generally don't need much space. Therefore, they get small tables in the rarified air of the Celeb Room alongside their contemporaries. These rooms get stuffy quickly, and the light – the light was simply awful. The larger Dealers' Room was located in a ballroom with high ceilings and chandeliers that could be dimmed to moody and flattering levels – unlike those nasty fluorescents that made a bad spell in rehab after the parts had dried up all the more regretful. Not only that, but Dealers' Room visitors were generally less nervous, which made for a more relaxed atmosphere – unless it were large crowds you feared. But as the good doctor eased his way into the vacillating current heading towards his table between the lobby card crew and the face painters, he couldn't for the life of him imagine why anyone with an aversion to crowds would bother turning up in the first place.

Eliza's legs had begun to ache badly. She knew that if she didn't at least try to make her way to a vertical position in the next couple of minutes, they would go numb, which meant excruciating pain when she was extracted from the stall by hotel security. Gods, the decision was so hard. When anxiety of the magnitude that she was experiencing was this relentless, one begins to wonder just how much damage one is willing to take. She was no closer to making her decision when what she knew was coming, finally came.

Knock-knock. The other stalls were surely occupied and someone had decided that the person in the one she was in didn't need to have a sit down when there were so many chairs, and if necessary, rug space available in the impressively large lobby. Fuck it, she thought. There's still an outside chance another stall will open up and whomever was out there would flow naturally to the area of lesser concentration.

"Umm...hello? Sorry."

The voice was sweeter than a ten-layer wedding cake – a black one, of course. She had seen one that Lily had printed out about a year ago and it got her to wondering "if". And even with that dagger of a memory slipping quietly into her heart, she was astonished at how instantly the woman's voice put her at ease. It had a bell-like, dulcet tone and a gentle lilt that was far from the zippy, assertive clip she was expecting. This wasn't your average conventioneer, that's for damn sure. That could only mean one of three things: there was also a baking convention in town and someone got the short straw when it came to choosing accommodations, there was an actress from one of the Celeb Rooms who'd had too much coffee and got tired of waiting for an elevator, or the person behind the cold, grey door was actually not a person at all but Glenda, The Good Witch, come to look for her greener sister and catching a glimpse of her twisted legs in the space between the door and the tile.

"I'm sick," Eliza muttered, confident that someone so nice wouldn't need any further explanation.

"Oh, honey...you want me to get you anything?" the voice replied.

"No...no, thanks."

Mercifully, whomever it was skipped away. She was wearing heels, from the sounds of it. Listening to them click along the floor sounded like long fingernails thrumming on the glass of a windowpane. Eliza would've felt bad about sending this woman's near to bursting bladder back out into the struggle if she hadn't been one-hundred percent certain that she felt one-hundred percent worse.

"Yoo-hoo!"

The voice was back. Eliza looked under the door to see a damp length of paper towel resting inside the most beautifully manicured hand she had ever seen.

"Try it on your forehead," said the voice. "That's what I do. If you don't want to mess up your makeup, try the back of your neck."

Eliza tried her forehead and felt better right away. Whether it was because of the cool temperature or the kind gesture she couldn't be sure. The next thing she knew, she was using the toilet rim for support as she lifted herself up and into a standing position. Ignoring the spell of dizziness that accompanied the effort, she fiddled with the lock and pulled open the door.

"Loretta?" Eliza couldn't believe how naturally the name danced across her chapped lips. Loretta was a character that gets horribly tortured in a film she had seen recently. Right when she manages to escape and make her way into the street, running with only one shoe on and screaming hysterically, she gets creamed by a tractor trailer. Oddly, she couldn't place the name of the film, but Loretta had been one of her favorites in it.

"Yep, it's me! I'm alive!" She made it sound so spontaneous. "And so are you! You want to give me two seconds and we'll get out of this joint?"

"Okay," Eliza said without thinking, "take your time."

"Perfect."

Loretta closed the door and Eliza could hear her shoes shuffling to achieve purchase on the tile in front of the bowl. Her sundress, colorful and kind to her rather big boned frame slid delicately down to her ankles making Eliza wonder if some people were born with the feminine wares of an angel or if they all had to work on them like she did. Suddenly she realized Loretta might still be able to see her shoes. Not wanting to appear pushy, she backed up into a little girl who was making a mess trying to wash her hands. Water was everywhere, and some of it was running to the stall where she had been. Loretta had saved her from wet ass. Was there no end to this woman's heroism?

"Okay, I'm done!"

Apparently the answer was "no". She had even bothered to announce her finishing up in order to reassure her. With that, the door swung open and Loretta emerged. Eliza was sure that a thimbleful of her pee was more valuable than everything she was selling at her table combined.

The two of them walked arm and arm out of the restroom and back into the melee. Loretta had enough star power to wedge them a safe path through the confusion. It was either that, or the guys stepped out of their way in response to some vestigial chivalrous instinct and/or to check her out. Eliza thought this must have been what it was like to attend a movie premier, or even a prom. She hadn't been to hers by choice, but she had no doubt this was better by several miles.

"By the way," her savior declared, "my real name is Lorena Downing."

"Eliza."

"Very nice to meet you, Eliza," she chimed, and added laughing, "even if it was in somewhat awkward circumstances. Feel free to call me Loretta if it's easier. Most people here do, and it's close enough, so fuck it."

The way the word "fuck" sounded out of her mouth, all "down" yet freakishly wholesome, almost made Eliza want to kiss her.

"You feel better, now," Lorena asked, "dealing with all this I mean?"

Eliza blushed. "Yeah, thanks...but how did you know I was having an anxiety attack?"

"Honey, let me tell you...you see how you were in there just a few minutes ago, curled up on the floor praying to die? That was me my first time, too. I love it now, but the first time I did one of these I'd only just finished a short run on *Days of Our Lives*. Eliza, I was petrified. Thank God I had my cell phone on me! I called my agent and she finally talked me down. Once I got some food back in me, I got into the groove and I was fine."

So that was it. She wasn't an angel at all, but a real person with real problems; problems not so far removed from her own. But that was surely where any similarities between them ended.

"So what were you in," Lorena chirped, "if you don't mind me asking? The scary stuff is new to me so I'm afraid I haven't seen all that much."

"Oh, I'm not an actress," Eliza said, correcting her.

Lorena cocked her head, and said, "You're not?

"I'm a dealer. I sell...stuff."

"Oh."

They had reached the entrance to the Dealers' Room and Lorena put on the breaks. Eliza hoped she hadn't disappointed her by being honest. Honesty was what actors prized most, wasn't it? In the glamorous world of a pretty actress it probably was, especially if you were getting paid for it, but not in the convention circuit. Here, someone would obviously favor a relationship with a fellow professional over a stupid girl who sold trinkets for pennies and probably threw up to stay skinny. She started to feel her nerves mumbling amongst themselves.

"Then this must be you!" Loretta was good. There wasn't a hint of disappointment in her sparkling green eyes.

"Yeah...this is me," mumbled Eliza. She inhaled slowly and deeply. The last thing she wanted was a hiccup to punctuate her heretofore already pathetic performance.

"Well, I'll have to stop by and see your goods next chance I get. What's the name of your company?"

"Once Bidden. We...I mean, I auction off authentic creature and monster artifacts." It sounded extra fucking stupid now.

"Ooh! That sounds so cool!" said Lorena, bouncing on her tip toes. "If you got any snips, snails and puppy dog tails save me some. I might want to make a love potion later." She leaned closer and whispered, "Dane Harding is one table over from mine."

Dane Harding was a cast-iron putz. Anyone with any knowledge of celluloid serial killers knew that his version of "Corporal Punishment", the infamous camouflaged stalker in the seventh through ninth installments of the *Landmine* series was easily the most forgettable. That probably went for the entire "Camo-Slasher" genre that had unfortunately established itself in recent years. He was a total cock in person, too. She had seen him be mean to a ten year-old kid who had mistaken him for Kelvin Tyne, the actor who portrayed "CP" in the first six films, and it literally made her smell bad eggs. He always made a show of standing up and stretching his steroid muscles whenever a cute girl showed up in line. Eliza was sure it was more to humiliate Tyne, who had lost most of his physique thanks to a motor cycle accident just after the shooting for *L:6* had wrapped, than an attempt to attract the opposite sex. She didn't want to spoil Lorena's excitement for fear that she might associate her with bad news, but she was ninety-five percent positive that the big douche bag was gay.

"I'm not sure I've got any of that stuff, but I'll see what I can do," Eliza said.

Lorena touched her shoulder and said, "Aww…you're such a doll."

She was, Eliza thought: a muddy and broken doll forgotten behind a trailer somewhere in Podunk, Nebraska – or any one of those artificial, punch line towns that people always made up.

"Alright," said Lorena, winding it down, "let me get back to my thing. If I don't get a chance to find you, you come find me, you hear?"

"Sounds good," Eliza replied, letting a commiserable gaze linger in her eyes for a beat too long.

"Sweet," said Lorena. "Okay…bye-bye."

And with a neat, pageant turn that reminded Eliza a little of her stepsister Maddie, Loretta was off to strut her way past "Corporal Punishment" on the way to a sparkling destiny. Eliza hoped she had made something of a lasting impression, at least enough to separate her from the rest of the litter. If she had, and the piteous expression didn't scare her away, maybe Lorena Downing would ditch the dick, and whisk her far, far away.

Dr. Dmitrije Radan signed his name on the inside cover of a copy of his latest *Dark Doctor* release with a fluid determination. He had just purchased a new pen in the gift shop and was pleased to find that he didn't need to press down at all in order to get a dark, solid line. The peaks of his arches and the bottoms of his loops were enigmatically pronounced, suspiciously virile and curiously alive, and they fit the tone of his novels perfectly. His central character was an evil physician with a simple, family practice, who manipulated his patients into serving his cursed and delinquent needs. Once he had procured those things he desired – anything from deviant sex to the bones of an infant that he would then sell into the black market for witchcraft – he would close up his office and move onto the next town. He was completely and utterly amoral, often taking the time to savor the chaos that he had caused before disappearing into the night. As a precaution, anyone who came into contact with him would forget ever having met him after being put under a hypnotic spell, save one hired assistant. He or she would usually be found strapped to a table in a mental asylum, replaying the events in their head that in turn made up much of the content of the book. The possibilities of new storylines were endless; as endless as the line of people that he now saw before him, all with books in hand and cash at the ready. He had become accustomed to the indefinite nature of his profession provided one, vital condition was met: that a significant number of his fans brought with them a vial of their own blood.

The vial of blood gimmick was something he employed for career longevity, much like his doctor character's hook, and one that made him a convention mainstay for as long as he had a use to be one. It went like this: each book bought off the table cost twenty-five dollars. These were for new books not yet released, and a deal with his publisher allowed him to name his price on a small, initial printing. If he signed one of them, it would cost fifty dollars. Most were happy to pay it. Of those who chose not to, half of them bought a book and left with it unsigned, and the other half bartered for his signature with a tiny bit of fresh blood.

It was all completely legal, and those who went that route were ecstatic about being in on the act. What Dmitrije found fascinating was not how many of them actually did it, but how few tried to fool him by using something like fake blood which could be easily obtained from any theme park magic shop. And not a one questioned his motives, for fear, he suspected, that they might supplant their own. Horror fan loyalty was as vehement and reliable as any he had encountered in all his days, and for those who sacrificed a small sample of their soul for the pleasure to believe he was selling their DNA on the black market, he made sure he used the new pen for a short note in their inscription. It was, he thought, the very least he could do.

He was moving along at a leisurely clip, managing to engage the more loquacious customer in polite conversation, when he began to feel a penetrating sensation somewhere in the soft palate on the roof of his mouth. It was as if he had continually bitten down on a thick piece of burnt toast, and the sharp crust had gnawed back at him. It was possible that he had eaten something that was too hot, so perhaps he had burned himself. Surely, if he had, he would have remembered—

"That's Chris, sir."

Dmitrije looked up to see a pleasant-looking young lad with a stained, button-down dress shirt and hair the color of lemon sorbet. He was reminding him whom the inscription was for, before continuing with his request for the note.

"*The doctor will see you now* would be rad," said Chris.

Dmitrije hadn't noticed that he had stopped writing as he examined the inside of his mouth, and it must have looked like he forgot what he was doing. Chris had wanted him to inscribe his book with the evil doctor's most famous line of dialog, something he must have written twenty times in the last half-hour alone.

"Of course, Chris," grinned Dmitrije.

He concentrated on his signature, doing his best to ignore the steady increase of discomfort that he had now taken to rubbing with his tongue. When he was finished, he gently closed the book and handed it to the boy's waiting hand.

"Thank you so much," he said, before looking back to the line and nearly shouting, "Next?"

Chris held his ground, reached into his shirt pocket and began fishing for something in between a few haunted hayride flyers he had stuffed there.

He produced a small vial of blood and held it out between his first and middle finger.

"Don't you want this?" he asked.

The vial caught a bit of incidental light and glistened invitingly in front of the celebrated author's face.

"Yes, of course." Dmitrije carefully removed the vial from between his fingers, surprised at how difficult it was not to snatch it in a feral flash, even if it meant breaking a few of the boy's digits in the process. He smiled, close lipped and wide, before sending him off with, "Thank you, again."

The boy, Chris, was clearly more sensitive than most boys his age. He had sensed Dmitrije's sudden edge, and retreated into the crowd unsure. Dmitrije almost felt sorry for him. It had nothing to do with the way he had asked for the inscription, or the way he had handed him his payment. That was not it at all. Dmitrije's change in mood had everything to do with what he now recognized as a migrating pain from a procedure performed on him several years ago. It was something he felt was necessary, like how one might remove the belongings of a lost loved one in order to block the agony of their absence. Only now, those personal effects had turned up when least expected and for no immediately apparent reason, leaving one to wonder how they got there and forcing them to face the anguish all over again.

Eliza breathed deeply through the neck of her hoodie as she walked towards her table. The initial influx of visitors had dissipated, making it easier to maneuver between the remaining dawdlers. As she did, she tried to pinpoint what exactly had caused her the anxiety attack so that maybe she could avoid it in the future. Was it the big crowds? She had never been claustrophobic or anything like that, and at one time enjoyed crowd surfing at concerts when Ryan dared her. Of course, everything was different now. Something in the very fabric of her being had changed, making her feel less human. She knew a few things for sure: it was extremely hard to breathe when she also had to speak, and when her body came into contact with someone else's – something as simple as a light rub of the shoulder – she wanted to cut that part off and throw it away. These facts, considering she was in the very place that usually made her feel the most comfortable, really started to worry her. So she decided that relegating them to the furthest recesses of her mind might be a good idea if she was to stay upright and away from the toilet. She had thought of having a shower upstairs in her room, but as quickly as the idea came she pushed it away. There were too many memories of Ryan associated with the intimacy of that space. To get to room 718, the room they had managed to book three years running, would mean taking a crowded and cramped elevator. Since the stairs weren't an option, that would have to wait indefinitely.

She squeezed her way between her table and the one next to it with all the belt buckles and leather goods, and took her place behind her merchandise. There were already several people fingering one item or another, and while six months ago she would have happily perceived this as business as usual, today she would love to have them all put down what they were holding and move along.

"How much to start the bidding?" said an extremely thin woman, about a head and a half taller than Eliza. She was holding up a baby werewolf pelt that had been an enormous score from an eBay seller named "Gravedigger". He or she had sworn up and down to its authenticity, and now, thinking back, it had been a huge mistake to cough up the eighty bucks plus shipping. Werewolves didn't have sex and make babies, and the likelihood of a baby being bitten and turned into a werewolf rather than just swallowed whole was extremely remote, even in the wildest of fantasies. Eliza had to admit that that was really what she was selling: fantasies. Which wouldn't have been such a crime had she not recently come to the conclusion that the very will to live was enough of a fantasy in itself.

"A hundred," answered Eliza. It seemed fair considering that it was probably just a muskrat skin. She might have gone for double that before, but unloading it at that price would give her double the cash she would need for the gas to get home.

"Hmm…I've only got eighty, she bargained. "And I know my friend was looking pretty hard at those teeth a few minutes ago. She did a quick scan of the room, never resting long enough in one place to really make out a face. "She's around here somewhere."

Eliza immediately folded and closed the bidding. Eighty bucks was eighty bucks and she knew she looked broke as a joke. And if there really was someone interested in the teeth, she might be able to jack up the price on them like she had originally planned. Out of everything she had on display, they looked the most real.

She reached across the shoebox full of harpy feathers, picked the teeth out of their two-by-two wooden box, and rolled them around in her hand. Nasty looking things, they were. Molted, pitted, chipped, about and inch and a quarter long including the root, and strangely cylindrical. She might've passed them off as a prehistoric drill bit if she wanted, but the new Eliza, the one with the rapidly waning interest in demonology of any kind, believed them to be pig's teeth. The unwritten rule of convention selling that Wendy had taught her on her first day was to pick something in your collection that looked cheap and make it the most expensive item on the table. Her reasoning was that, if something so awful was so valuable, it made the nicer stuff seem more of a steal. You probably wouldn't sell it, but that's good because you really wanted to keep it – unless someone offered you, like, a million dollars or something. She advised her to put them under glass, too, and maybe even spring for a small spotlight to shine on them. As it was, the hideous things were her centerpieces, but she had only managed to find a semi-cool, hand carved wooden box to put them in. The old Eliza had enough light in her to make anything seem fabulous. Today, had she the energy, she might have listened to Wendy and bought a cheap penlight from the gift shop. Now was the time to do it, too, as a lot of the dealers were closing early for some reason and the place was emptying out pretty quickly.

Rufus, bless his heart, took advantage of the lull by trotting his way over.

"Where'd you go?" he panted, trying to catch his breath from his twenty-foot jog. "I almost came looking for you."

"You wouldn't have found me, trust me."

"Everything cool? No one's giving you any trouble, are they? He puffed out his chest. "Cause if they are, I'll give them a great price on a dirt nap."

He really was trying, she admitted to herself. If it were to eventually get her up to his room, he would fail miserably, but if she were using her heightened sensitivity to all things human, he would have passed with flying blacks.

"No, I'm okay," she assured him. "I just sold a pelt for eighty bucks."

"You're amazing, you know that? Some people barely have to get out of bed in the morning to make money."

He was trying to make her feel better, but if this had been the old Eliza, he would have only succeeded in pissing her off. Basically what he was saying was that she looked like shit. Only, old Eliza would have known better and they probably wouldn't even be having this conversation at all.

"Thanks," she replied politely. "How's it going over there?"

"Shitty," he shrugged, "but I don't care. If I make back my rental and libation tab you know I'm happy. In fact, a bunch of us are thinking about packing it in early. Mostly everyone here's macking on celebs and our people don't really show up until tomorrow."

He was fidgeting nervously, and had taken to sweeping away a forelock that was neither in his eyes nor willing to stay where he wanted it.

"Right," Eliza said.

"So, you wanna?"

"Drink?" Food was a better idea, but his offer did make her wonder if she needed to take a few more pills. "No, thanks. I think I'm just going to stay here and count my two twenties, one ten, five fives, four ones, and four quarters." She was good at counting money, no matter how fucked up her head was.

"Now that that's done," he said, "how 'bout it?"

"No, Francis, you go ahead," she nearly pleaded. "I'm fine, promise."

"Okay, *Lies*," he said, jabbing her one last time. "I'll be back to check on you."

He followed out a few guys in Freddie Kruger costumes and broke into a run once he hit the lobby. It may have looked to the untrained eye like he was getting away from her as quickly as he could, but she knew he was only hurrying to take advantage of all the drinks that would be bought for him if he got in on the round. Run, Rufus, run.

She put the teeth back into their box, tucked the quarters under a stack of Once Bidden flyers she had printed but neglected to put out, and stuffed her fist of cash into her hoodie pocket. It was a good start all things considered, and the money in her hand made her feel a little more like the hell she was enduring was worth it.

Friday

part three

Dmitrije was thankful for the break. The aching in his mouth had eased off a bit, only to be replaced by a cramp in his right hand. Soon, he would check his phone for messages from his agency and decide if he would return them. They needed him more than he needed them at this point, but he kept them on because it meant he only needed to talk to one person instead of twenty in order to get a book on the market. In fact, real conversation was rarely necessary. Text messaging a "no" or a "yes", and the occasional "one more week" was all that he usually needed to do. And face-to-face meetings, unless they made the time to get in line at a convention, were all but non-existent.

Writing novels had proven a wise choice for a new vocation. The only thing that had made him more money and given him more freedom was black market trading of prescription medication, but the illegality of it had required some very bothersome relationships that he was more than happy to do without. However, he wasn't sorry he had spent the thirteen years making them, as they had given him all the information and material he needed to write his books. Of course, there were a host of other activities a solitary creature like him could have done to survive, but he had always enjoyed a certain amount of finer things, acquired the way most things were acquired: by paying for them. Being upstanding had its benefits, and taking part in the obliging system of American capitalism was one of them.

He tucked his money into the inside pockets of his jacket, splitting the amount in half so as to maintain the fine balance of his present disposition. The vials, eleven in total, he slipped into a leather pouch before zipping it closed. There were convention staff conveniently spaced throughout the room to keep an eye on inventory, and they were well trained. He never had to say a word to them. All he had to do was simply rise out of his chair, and one or more of them would take a cheating step towards him. If he were just loosening his back, they would retake their previous positions. If he took one step around to the front of the table, they would wordlessly negotiate and the winner would stand watch. He had to hand it to them. Regardless of the inherent honor one could credit to the average horror fan, there was always one who ruined it for everybody and his rented guardians used this knowledge – or paranoia, perhaps – exceedingly well.

Dmitrije stood out of his chair, pouch in hand, and stepped into the fair game zone. He referred to it as such because once you freed yourself from the confines of your professional space, you gave implied permission to be approached, photographed, and in some cases, physically embraced. The suit jacket normally neutralized the latter danger, but the first two were conclusively in attendance. This would only be more the case once the first wave of visitors had returned from the hotel bar with loosened inhibitions, and he was determined to make the elevator before that happened. Now seemed a good time to take his chances.

As he glided past the embattlements and passed through the exit, he felt another pang. It didn't last long, but it left a lingering tingle that couldn't be ignored. He was fully aware of what it was now, and past experience told him to seek out whomever was tickling his anterior mandibular senses before he found himself in an awkward situation. The pain was an indication of a powerful amount of negative energy in close proximity. It was one of the unique attributes of his chosen state that few had ever really understood. So much of the mythology was antiquated silliness, and frankly, he liked it that way. It was better to be a straw man. But he, like every other organism in the room, had come to their survival instincts by way of some manner of adaptation. For example, scientists were finally beginning to better understand the nature of some of history's most notorious predators.

The Tyrannosaur, for example, was long thought to be an aggressive hunter. Films had been made where fleeing vehicles were chased down by the hulking beast at speeds of up to fifty miles per hour. It was, he believed, pure nonsense. T-Rex was a vicious and unmerciful predator, that much was correct, but the current prevailing theories about his hunting habits made him out to be more like a giant vulture that happened upon the kill of another animal and took his turn without asking. His kind, Dmitrije posited, had come to similar conclusions. The weak and injured, in this case emotionally and spiritually, were the easiest of prey. Why run when you can walk? Why sprint, when you can stalk? So with this thought in mind, the room relatively empty, and by his calculations still a few seconds to spare, he made the decision to have a stroll.

As he surveyed the aisles, he paid careful attention to those in his immediate vicinity. This was most unwise if you were seeking to be left alone. In his case, it may appear as if he were eager to engage everyone around him in a discussion about their ambitions to become a writer. A few years ago, at a poorly attended event due to repeated hurricane warnings, he had chosen to take a lap out of sheer boredom. Half way around he made the mistake of asking someone a question about a book they had in their bag. Before he knew it he had become a student of Wallachian bark, which apparently cured everything from rheumatism to lycanthropy. This time, he adopted a look of mild concern, as if addressing a pressing matter that could only be assuaged by locating just the person he was looking for. So far it was working, which allowed his faculties to direct him.

He was getting closer to the source.

Eliza pulled her hood over her head, folded her arms and laid face down on top of them. She had begun to feel nauseous again, but this time it was more down to lack of food. It was an annoying, biological purgatory to withstand when her body was hungry yet she had no appetite. Maybe if Wendy or Francis came back she would ask them to grab her something. She was more likely to eat if she could pick at something behind her table than if she actually had to go and sit down with – *gasp* – other people.

With her retinas focused on the undulating circles of light beneath her eyelids, she sensed someone standing at her table. It was possible they had stopped to do any number of things that had nothing to do with her. They could be looking in their bag to see if they had dropped something. They could be checking their watch, or a text message. They could have found themselves a little lost, and stopped to get their bearings. Any one of those options would do. What wouldn't do was someone insisting on asking her a question when it was pretty fucking obvious that she had taken down her shingle. For each instance, ignoring their presence was the appropriate response and that was exactly what she intended to do.

"Sorry to bother you," said the voice, this time distinguished and male, "but may I?"

Fuck off, she thought to herself. The lights in her eyes were popping like road flares.

"I'll tell you what," the voice continued, "you keep resting and I'll help myself. You have my word not to run off with anything and if I'm interested, I'll simply leave you the money for my bid, and be on my way. Stay just as you are, and I'll know it's a deal."

She hadn't thought of that option at all, yet it seemed so simple. She could have just made a sign to the effect of the honor system he was suggesting and taken her chances sleeping in the car. It probably would have been loads better for business than sitting there like she was now, repelling people with her attitude. His voice had a theatrical cadence that made her feel as though she was in a dream, which also appealed. It was a voice she might be able to trust, so per the deal, she chose not to move. Only now, she kind of wanted to see what he looked like.

"Very well," he said, without the slightest hint of irritation, "now...what do we have here?"

Whoever it was wasn't going to go away. In fact, it sounded like they were going to pull every passive aggressive method known to man to get her full and undivided attention. Resigned to her defeat, she raised her head, pulled off her hood, and looked up. It was the book guy. She'd forgotten the name of them...Doctor *Something.* He had been signing copies and was hidden behind a wall of people for pretty much the entire evening – well, as far as she knew. She had her head in a toilet for much of it.

"There you are!" he said with mock surprise. "Does this mean the deal's off?"

"No," said Eliza. "Do what you want."

"Alright," he agreed.

He reached down, picked up the vampire teeth, and held them in the air as if to determine if they were transparent.

"How much might a set of these beauties set me back? And be honest. Don't go easy just because I'm an old man."

"You're not an old man." She knew he was fishing, so she cut to the chase. Getting on with this was her first priority, not puffing up some old book guy's ego.

"My dear...anyone who looks like I do and is interested in purchasing teeth most certainly qualifies as an old man." He rocked from one foot to the other with a bit of showmanship. "I believe it's written there in your convention handbook." He inspected her eyes. "Ah...you haven't bothered to read the handbook, have you?"

"I don't need a handbook," she boasted. There was no harm in playing along, but he was starting to wear a little.

"Then how much to take them home now, hmm?" He pulled a money clip from his front pocket, and theatrically thumbed through the bills. "Fifty? Sixty?"

"Three-hundred."

"I hope you're talking dinar," he responded.

"Sorry," barked Eliza.

She reached up and took the teeth from the tips of his fingers. She hadn't moved that fast in as long as she could remember.

"Try dollars, mister," she wisecracked. "If it's too steep, I'm sure there's plenty here that will suit your budget."

Eliza saw the book guy chuckle. It reminded her of how Ryan reacted when they were arguing and he wanted it to stop. He knew he didn't want to hurt her, so it became absurd at some point, which caused him to laugh. The thought instantly depressed her, so she sat back and frowned.

Dimitrije reached up to his mouth and touched it as if to acknowledge it was there. But it was the pain inside that had made him react without thinking. The girl had him off guard. She was clearly in a state of debilitating torment, yet she was trying her best to conceal it. It was the most charming thing he had seen in ages. And she hadn't so much as blinked when he mentioned "dinar".

Eliza broke the silence. "Listen, if you want them…for real, I'm saying—"

"No, no, no…don't you dare lower your prices for me. To be honest, I'd say three-hundred dollars was a bargain." He was starting to sound like Santa Claus when only a few minutes earlier he had thought of crushing a young boy's hand. There was something about her, something that spoke to him that he couldn't quite place. There was no need to spend this much time softening her up, not that he was intending on doing anything untoward. He had made the trip around simply to identify who was causing his face a bit of bother. Now, he was chatting for the sake of chatting. Why?

"A bargain, huh? You some kind of expert?" At least she could get some feedback from a seasoned pro. If he really thought three-hundred bucks was too low, maybe she could unload them and get the hell out of there.

"As a matter of fact, I'm not. But I'd wait a bit longer just in case you get a better offer. It's only Friday, and you never know." He checked his watch. "Now, I have to get to my room and freshen up before dinner. But before I go, I'd like to know your name, if I may."

"Eliza." Her answer was perfunctory and serviceable. As far as she was concerned, she was delivering information that would facilitate further business, not agreeing to an introduction.

"Dr. Dmitrije Radan, Eliza…it's been a pleasure."

He smiled a wide, close-lipped smile and closed the pig's teeth in her hand. His fingers felt a little plastic and unreal, she noted, but at least she didn't want to cut away the part he touched.

"See you around," he said, with a little vaudeville flair. Then he gave a tiny bow, backed away, and was gone.

Eliza nearly winced at his goodbye. At least it came off totally innocent, or so she hoped. She *really* didn't need a stalker right now.

Dmitrije exited the elevator at the 18th floor, took the first right at the ice machine, and silently counted off the remaining three doors until he reached his room. A practiced insertion of his room key activated the tiny green light that told him he could finally relax his expression of mild distress, and allow it to settle into what he was really feeling: deep concern. Only, for the first time in some time, it wasn't just for himself.

He switched on the light in the bathroom that was located right near the door, walked towards the desk that held some of his personal effects and added his pouch to them. He removed his jacket, placed it on the back of the chair and sat on the edge of the bed, loosening his neck and making small circles with his ankles. The ache in his mouth had disappeared, leaving behind the persistent tingle that made it seem as though he had wired one of his fillings to a 9-volt battery hidden in his shirt pocket. He decided not to turn on the main light in the room, this time, preferring the ambient light of the bathroom. It provided him a haven of sorts where he could hide. Hiding in one's own room was another sign, he realized, of an internal conflict that he had been waging for several years now. However, that battle would have to wait if he were to get through the weekend. For now, it was time to do what he really came in to do.

He reached out to the desk, grabbed the pouch, and opened it carefully. He could hear the satisfying sound of glass rubbing against glass as the vials succumbed to his fingers squeezing them this way and that. He looked to the ceiling and placed his fingers inside the pouch, removing one of the vials as if removing one of those little numbered white balls that they used for the state lottery. He promised himself years ago that he wouldn't allow himself to fall into the habit of prioritizing his selection. When he did that, he ran the risk of obsessing on which vials he could afford to *expend*, and those that he preferred to *reserve*. In some ways it had become a game. In other ways it was very much ritualized behavior meant to manage a very real condition, but that interpretation was for another time when he was playing doctor. Today he was an author of fiction, and a game would more than suffice.

He deposited the vial that he had chosen into a soft gully in the bed comforter and zipped the pouch closed. The pouch was placed into the tiny refrigerator located next to the desk. Returning to the chosen vial, he held it in front of his face and studied it. The clear, screw top container was fairly common and could easily be purchased online by those who had done a small amount of research. How the blood was transferred into the vial made him curious, but he knew better than to ask. He imagined most would simply prick their fingers and squeeze what they could into the vial before closing it – not exactly “class one” clean room conditions. He hadn’t tried it himself, but now and again he would wonder if one hole in the finger was enough to fill the tiny, two-milliliter enclosure. He couldn’t imagine how those who sold the vials in bulk could live with themselves knowing that most of them wound up on the ground in lower-economical neighborhoods all across America. Further investigation stopped there, however, before too many parallels were drawn and he became lost in the grey fog of subjective morality.

He twisted the tiny black cap off of the top, and held onto it. This wouldn’t take forever and he found that replacing it immediately was the best way to dispose of it. With an almost dainty precision, he brought the vial to his mouth and rested the opened end onto his lower lip. He remembered how, the first time, he had felt a little like Gulliver sharing a toast with one of the Lilliputians. He had to admit that it held a similar significance. He was a giant of sorts, drinking to his health, with the fate of some very little people at his fingertips. With a combination pour and suck, he withdrew the blood from the vial and transferred it onto his tongue. Its metallic piquancy coated his taste buds and he let a bit of it run down into the sublingual well – the same place where a heart patient might place a drop of nitroglycerin. A rush of warm energy flooded into each one of his limbs.

Immediately he thought of the one he loved so long ago. He touched her stomach with one hand and palmed one of her breasts with the other. She was on top of him, her hair hiding her eyes and shielding her hunger. She pushed down onto him, impaling her dripping softness, drinking to *her* health and taking from him what *she* needed. And then she was gone. He had learned how much of their past together he could revisit each day. He might try again later, this time remembering a laugh as she pressed her lips to his, but that would depend on how much he was willing to risk the tempest that always followed. The sliver of time between the taste of his tincture and what he became seconds after was the only rift he could slip through that assured him safe return.

For that reason, it was very precious. It was the last bit of sun on the horizon just before it dipped below the earth, the final moments of a spark, or the tragically brief life of a snowflake just before it melted in your hand. In that fleeting moment there could be her, but then she had to go.

Eliza watched with growing apprehension as the dealers packed up what they would be taking with them to their rooms. It was important to be careful about what you chose. Once the doors were locked, they would not be opened again until the next morning. She had found a bearable stasis behind her booth, and the thought of having to relocate to somewhere besides the bathroom stall made her very anxious. Francis had not come back at all, which didn't surprise her. She figured he had said he would check up on her to ease his departure, but maybe that wasn't fair. She remembered how things used to get wonderfully out of control once the drinks started to flow, and how steadily the time slipped away with each melting ice cube. However, for her, the last few hours of the day were brutal to say the least. She spent them organizing her inventory until everything that was on the left side of the table was now on the right and vice versa. A few last minute shoppers had stopped to watch her do it, and she could tell they were waiting for her to relax so they could ask her a question. That was why she took her time. Now that they had moved on, she was faced with a couple of choices: one, find Wendy and see if she wanted to get something to eat; two, go to her car, grab her bag and take it up to the room; or three, go to her car and stay there.

The night had somehow become warmer than the day, which was a phenomenon she knew to be practically synonymous with central Florida. Whatever cold front had passed through was long gone, and even though the sun had dropped out of the sky twenty minutes ago, normal, muggy service had resumed. Charging the air was that buzz that always accompanied the first night of a convention. People were loading up their cars with some of the stuff they had bought or had signed, and rushing back in to start partying in their rooms. Those who knew how to do it right booked a block of rooms together on the same floor, and ducked in and out of each other's spaces which were often designated as the "movie room", the "bar", the "game room", and of course, the "sex room". When she and Ryan had first started coming to the conventions, she was shocked to find that everyone had a "sex room", but it really should have been called the "personal items" room, or "the place where you stored the stuff you didn't want stolen" room. It comforted her that hardly anyone she knew or knew of used the convention solely as an opportunity to hook up. Sure, it happened, but probably not with any more regularity than with your average convention crowd. After all, she had met Ryan here, and they had shared room 718 all weekend. There she was, as slut-for-Satan as she could pull off, and he all brooding and just-this-side of Goth-industrial rock god. Neither one of them touched the other for all three days, until the very last moment when he had given her a kiss on both cheeks. See, dad?

Now, she was alone, walking as quickly as her suffering body would let her to where her Neon was parked. The parking lot, large as it was, seemed ten times as large as she remembered it. She fumbled around with the keys in her pocket to eat up some of her nervous energy, and started pressing the fob about twenty feet further than the car could hear it. Eventually, the headlights blinked hello, and she dove into the front like she was hiding from a helicopter.

Inside, the quiet felt soothing, like sleep. She hadn't eaten anything since she threw up, and wondered just how much nutritional value there was in a single, round pill. She could always avoid the crowds in the restaurant by purchasing a few energy bars in the gift shop, so maybe that was what she would do. But first, always first, she needed to feed the beast.

She dug into the hand-painted *FrankenBarbie* purse she had bought from another eBay store. It sported the green head of Barbie, in profile, with a bolt in her neck. She loved it when she saw it, and thought it would go well with her hoodie. She still sort of liked it, but it had never looked more functional and less of a statement than it did at that moment. She followed the rattling sound of the pill container and pulled it from the forgotten dregs of the bag's contents. It made her sick how fast she was moving to get those pills in her mouth, but by now she was on autopilot. A quick press and twist of the cap, and there they were: waiting at the bottom of the brown, plastic bottle. A couple of shakes later, and three – better make it four – of the little white discs slid into her hand like excited toddlers caterpillaring off a sliding board. She didn't even have anything to wash them down except her own spit. It would work, she thought, as she threw them back and swallowed hard. Once they were down, there was nothing left to do but screw the cap back on, drop them back into her purse, and wait until the storm's electricity found her lightening rod and Dr. Frankenstein pronounced her alive again.

"Dmitrije?"

The voice coming through the door was from a woman whose first language was clearly not American English. Why would someone bother him, he wondered. Anyone who needed to speak with him could do so by two different phones. He hadn't called for housekeeping, not that he remembered, and he knew he wasn't making any noise lying on his bed with his shoes off, staring at the blank ceiling.

And why were they using his first name?

He rolled onto his feet, a thoroughly incensed man. He was angrier than he thought he could ever still be. Angrier, perhaps, than that day over a decade ago when he had made the decision to put his pain on ice so that he might survive long enough to determine if surviving was worth it. As it was, he was the man he was today because he made some careful considerations about how he wanted to live the remainder of his time on earth. First and foremost, he wanted to be someone who would move forward with a purpose. So he made some *adjustments*. His knack for fiction had helped him choose, and his affinity for darkness – along with his immeasurable anger – had fine-tuned that choice. There wasn't much time, he recalled, to research options beyond what he had already understood. The opportunity had presented itself, so he had taken it. Had he taken the other, he would not have been in that hotel room, wandering through the dark, one hand searching for the doorknob. In fact, he would not have been anywhere at all, or so his atheistic leanings would have him believe.

He turned the knob and pulled open the door. Just as he had gotten it halfway open, he had an inkling as to who it was. Once it was fully open, his premonition had been confirmed. It was a woman, all right. Someone he had just visited in his mind, and it was from there that she was calling him. Damn it, he thought. This utter vexation – one that always accompanied a vial session and the reason he sat alone in the dark for at least twenty-minutes afterward – had let her overstay her welcome. Now he would have to try and do something to send her on her way again.

Dmitrije strode out of the elevator and into the lobby, which was full of the raucous echoes of those who had been indulging in spirits while he was upstairs summoning spirits of his own. He had changed into a navy blue sweater, and hoped that no one would notice him sneak in and take a seat on a little couch in the back, out of the way of the action. A waitress saw him, however, and quite by accident he did an impression of Peter Lorre in *M* and ordered a coffee before changing it quickly to brandy. He still enjoyed a drink – a real drink – now and again. He had been thoughtful enough not to excise every human custom from his repertoire, and that included food. He couldn't really taste much outside of strong, preferably sweet liquids and foods with lots of sugar. But in order to keep in step with the rest of society, he indulged when he felt it was appropriate.

He thought about his slip up in the room earlier. He had dropped his guard without realizing it. In the back of his mind he knew why, but he still wanted to go through the customary checks. The blood didn't taste tainted in any way, and was without a doubt that of a human being. He had chosen the vial quite by random, and there hadn't been any loud noises or sudden bursts of light with which to contend. It could only have been her: the young girl from the Dealers' Room. He had felt her from the off and still felt her now. Somehow she had contaminated his vision, rattled his concentration. He felt her more strongly now then he did in the room, but she wasn't in the lobby and she certainly wasn't doing shots with the guys in the werewolf masks. He supposed he could still be shaken from the experience upstairs, but it was highly unlikely. At least the anger was subsiding, which was a good thing. Had it headed in the other direction, something that hadn't happened in many years, there wouldn't be many happy faces in that restaurant for sure.

He finished his brandy and sensed that they were about to close the bar, which meant the elevators would soon be full. He felt the liquor warm his body, but that could have easily been from his wearing a sweater in a room so charged with energy – something he was rapidly losing. He accepted that he would have to wait until tomorrow to see the girl, even before he accepted that she was the reason he had come down in the first place. It was all getting too fuzzy, so he signed his room number on the check and slipped away.

Eliza watched as groups of people – two, three, four at a time – scurried past her car unaware that there was anyone in it. She liked that feeling. She liked thinking that she wasn't there, yet still able to see the world around her. Again, she was invisible. Of all the superpowers, that would be the one she would choose. She had not been crazy about heights since she was a little girl; a fall off the roof of her dad's van saw to that. And she didn't think that being super strong afforded her anything all that interesting. But to be invisible appealed greatly to her sense of curiosity and entitlement. Why shouldn't she be able to go wherever she wanted and hear what people were saying? Why all the secrets? Maybe that's why she started Once Bidden with Ryan in the first place. It was kind of their way at getting back at the world for having the answers but not sharing them. All she wanted to do was live her life, mind her own business, watch horror films and love her boyfriend. It couldn't have been any more simple that that. She certainly didn't have any answers now, only this time, she knew there weren't any. That was the worst part. That was the part that made being invisible no longer something she desired. Now, it wasn't unseen she wanted to be, but *unbeen*. She wanted to disappear entirely.

Lies and Love leaned back in her seat, shut her eyes and waited. Whether it was for the pills to kick in or for her wishes to be granted, she didn't care. At this point, either would do.

Saturday

part one

Eliza was awakened by a knock on her window. She cracked one eyelid just enough to make out her friend Wendy looking down at her, shielding her eyes with her hands so she could see inside. It was like she was shouting with her face.

"Eliza, what are you doing out here? Did you sleep here? Don't tell me you slept here!" They were questions to be asked and never answered. Wendy knew damn well that she hadn't been to her room as every Saturday since her first convention Wendy called her – them, to be technical – for breakfast. Eliza had forgotten that detail, but it wasn't as if there was anything she would have done about it. It would have been just another piece of information she would have happily chased away with her pills, several of which she was in dire need.

"What time is it?" croaked Eliza. She wanted to move the conversation on to something practical. And she did kind of want to know.

"Ten, I think," said Wendy. "Are you coming in?"

Eliza thought about telling her that she wasn't sure in a preemptive effort to avoid any future short term plans.

"I'm coming," she said, dismissively. "See you inside."

"Okay," said Wendy. "See you."

Wendy headed back in, as well meaning as anyone has ever been. Eliza, on the other hand, meant only to dig into her purse.

* * *

Dmitrije stood in front of the mirror and buttoned his dress shirt with leisurely precision. The vial he blind picked this morning was of a surprisingly high volume, and he had needed an hour of slowly ripping apart the telephone book followed by a half-hour in a freezing cold shower to calm down. He may have frightened the housekeeper as well, who walked in on him "decompressing". In an attempt to smooth things over, he cleaned up the shreds of phone book and placed them neatly inside the wastepaper basket so that when the woman returned – *if* she returned after being so coldly berated – she wouldn't have to do it.

He slipped out into the hall, and noticed the high number of trays set out in front of nearly every single room save his own. Late night room service – he thought with a sense of camaraderie – was less like eating and more like feeding. He could relate. After he had chosen to become what he now was, he hadn't seen many differences between himself and the average human being. We are all driven by unflattering urges at times, and now more than ever, people lead full and prosperous lives at all hours of the twenty-four hour day. Sure, he couldn't enjoy something like a glass of wine like he used to, but how many people even like wine or any of the other things that were now off his personal menu? He had to admit that his dependency on an elusive substance made him appear less dignified and more like a common addict if one chose to look at it in that way. But what of diabetics and others who suffer from potentially debilitating ailments? And what of those among them who weren't able to get the medication they needed because it wasn't available or they couldn't afford it? He had seen the result of hundreds of people – people in his own care – who were denied life-saving drugs simply because they disagreed politically with those who had plenty of them. He held them as they questioned the very idea of humanity through receding gums and sallow cheeks. For one of them – *her* – he would have given his own life so that she might be spared, but it wouldn't have done any good. His death could not have saved her, and her life meant nothing if lived in chains. So when it had come time to choose whether he still wished to remain a textbook representative of humankind, he didn't need very long to make his decision. And outside of a few minor incidents that could have seen him locked away in a mental institution, he hadn't regretted it one bit.

He walked to the elevator and pressed the down button. A new craving had begun to work its way into his heart like a snake that refused to be banished by the words of a spurious saint. And he was going down as far as he needed to satiate it.

Eliza received her change from the gift shop cashier, and pulled the plastic bag that held her items from the counter.

"Is that all you're having?" Wendy nagged. "An energy bar?"

Wendy had understood her situation and been kind enough to let her use her shower. While she felt better now, at least in the cleanliness department, showering had turned out to be something of an ordeal. The pills had kicked in early, possibly because she was still under the effects of the four she had taken the night before, and she slipped while bending over to squeeze the suds out of her hair. She received a lump on her head for her trouble, but she didn't tell Wendy. Their bond had taken on a creepy mother-daughter vibe and she needed to leave the nest as soon as possible.

"One bar's good for now," Eliza reassured her. "It's easy enough to get another one if I need it."

"Okay, well, I don't have time to argue with you. This rich-looking guy is supposedly coming back to pick up one of my ceramic skull flower pots and I got the feeling he wanted to commission some more. You'll meet me for lunch, then?"

"Yes," she agreed. "Just...if I'm busy, don't wait for me, k?"

Eliza could tell Wendy knew she was planning on blowing her off, but it got them both off the hook for the time being.

"I love you." She kissed her on the forehead and floated out.

Eliza watched her go, and got a thought: was it a surefire sign one was on a downward spiral if people were always walking away? It probably was.

She flipped up her hoodie and made her way out of the gift shop, weaving in and out of the human traffic that stood between her and the Dealers' Room. It was getting close to noon, and she was thankful that the day, in astrological terms at least, was half over. Hopefully, her little plan would work, and she could kill the rest of the time sitting in the dark upstairs in one of the movie rooms. If while she were there the day was cut to ribbons like a hapless co-ed at an abandoned summer campsite, she would thank her lucky stars and walk away with her take. What that take would be was totally dependent on the efficacy of the system she had devised yesterday; right after that book guy had left. And already $74.39 into the $300 she would need to cover her rent and travel expenses, she felt like she could afford risking a few hours testing it.

It had taken only a few minutes to get back to her table. Mostly everyone had broke for lunch or had gone back up to their room to stash their swag. The pills were still working nicely, and she perked up in anticipation of melting into the darkness of the makeshift theater on the second floor. If she had read the poster correctly, they would be showing *The Lost Boys* at one o'clock. If they were, she would be vanishing into the Hollywood town of Santa Carla inside twenty minutes.

She reached into the gift shop bag and took out the loose-leaf notebook she bought along with the $1.79 red Sharpie and started writing on one of the pages. The words **GHOST AUCTION,** in all capital letters, ran from one side of the page to the other. She was pleased with how evenly she had managed to space out the letters so that the words fit neatly in the center framed by tidy, one-inch margins. She ripped the page out, set it aside and began writing on the next. The sentence **WRITE YOUR BID UNDER THE NAME OF THE ITEM YOU WANT**, required the use of an entire sheet of paper, and she had to squeeze in the word **WANT** a little. Still, it was legible, and there was no escaping what she was asking them to do. If someone wanted to buy, for example, her collection of harpy feathers, they would write down their bid into the space provided on the sheet of paper she planned to assign to each item and either move onto another bid or go about their business elsewhere. She ripped out a third piece of paper and wrote: **BIDDING CLOSES @ 5PM**. This was negotiable, but she needed to give them a time constraint so that they wouldn't dilly-dally until it was too late to up their offer. Underneath the time she added: **Once Bidden Will Announce the Winners and Collect Payment**, and in parentheses **(No Show and The Item Will Be Awarded to the Next Highest Bidder)**. She arranged the signs neatly in the center of the table, and placed the

Sharpie in the middle of the one that told them when the bidding would be over. With a final thought, she snapped up the Sharpie and wrote **Low Reserves!** under the words **GHOST AUCTION**. It screwed up the vertical balance a little, but she figured they would get over it. Then, as a final touch, she placed starting bid prices next to the name of each item on tiny, ripped-out sections of paper. She wasn't asking a king's ransom, but if she managed to get the reserve price for everything it would make up the difference that she needed.

Old Eliza would have thought her "ghost auction" idea was completely insane. First of all, there was too much trust involved. Forget the chance of someone stealing an item; someone could steal the pen! Depending on bidders to have their own pen would be pushing it, and it was pushed damn near off the cliff already. Also, Old Eliza could have guaranteed the $225.61 she needed out of the sale of her least desirable inventory alone, but she still wouldn't have settled for it. She would rather pack it up than give it away, because she knew that meant it was worth more at the next convention when the same cheap-ass loser came around for another browse. Still, what she would end up banking at the convention and from subsequent sales on her eBay store (which hadn't worked in months) would completely eliminate her need for a second source of income. New Eliza, poor thing, was counting on today's totals, whatever she could guilt out of her dad, and a pain pill "scrip" that was due to run out in a few weeks. Soon, she was going to have to figure out a way to make a paycheck, and the concept was so daunting it made her lightheaded just thinking about it.

She shook off the thought and filled out all the price tags. A last "once over" and she was holding her arms close to her sides and worming her way through the crowds to the exit. It had now gotten to the point that she could do it without Rufus seeing her – the Rufus in the room, that is. She always hoped that the one in outer space chasing satellites was looking down and watching her when he took a break.

Which had become more tedious: signing or chatting? Dmitrije pondered this question as he reached for his next book. He thought he noticed the insipid chat at first, but there was no doubt that the jotting down of meaningless epithets to people he didn't know was rapidly making ground. His wrist hurt, an indication that he was slightly "undernourished" and he was now sitting next to a small pile of his novels – six, seven perhaps – that he had ruined by either getting the name wrong or just forgetting how to spell. Ever since he had seen the girl leave – Eliza, it was – he had been distracted. He had done a grand job of hiding it, though. It was then he discerned that hiding how he really felt had overtaken the other two activities in the death race towards utter banality.

He looked down the line and guessed that there were at least a good half-hour's worth of signing left to do. He mentally counted about four vials collected since he had begun this morning – which, if his calculations were correct, brought the total to thirteen minus those he had already ingested and discarded. At about two a day – one in the morning, and one at approximately five in the afternoon – he clipped along at an unhurried pace. Sitting around didn't sap too much energy; although he had a feeling this preposterous pining he was doing was taking its toll. So, in an effort to maintain the status quo – which meant leaving the convention with ten vials in total – he would have another four and a half days until he needed more blood. If that weren't possible, he would put his body into more frequent resting states until he thought of something. He could call his agent and have her set up a signing somewhere, which was feasible, or see if they got that mail-order deal happening. All the meetings had been taken and the milestones set and met, so it was entirely within the realm of possibility that he would go home to several refrigerated containers of the vital fluids waiting for him. So in theory, and with a little good fortune, he could call it a day right then and there. He inspected the last person in line: she was black, looked uncomfortably warm in an ivory, Medieval chemise, and was reluctantly agreeing to something a young boy, presumably hers, wanted her to buy for him.

Dimitrije leaned over towards one of the convention staff and said, "After her in the white dress-looking thing, I'm taking a break."

The greatest vampire film ever made – as far as Eliza was concerned – hadn't started yet. A few people had beaten her to the pick of the seats, but they had foolishly chosen the very front. Through a stiff neck and several migraines she had learned not to sit too close to the screen. If the projector had been set up hurriedly like everything usually is, parts of the screen would be slightly out of focus. The closer you were, the more chance you had of being stuck with a fuzzy view. All the way in the back opened up your angle possibilities, and dodgy focus was hardly ever an issue. Also, sitting close never worked for her in terms of making something scarier. It wasn't the film that gave her the creeps; it was usually the collective tension in the crowd that did it. For a film like *The Lost Boys,* she was more interested in laughing at the Coreys and wishing she were Jamie Gertz than being scared, and it didn't even matter if her character were a vampire at the time or not. Either would slake her thirst for otherness, invulnerability and a life lived eternally in the past. That's what she wanted: to stay forever in a rerun. If someone gave her the choice to cut out a piece of her life that would replay forever, or even just every once and awhile, she would bite his or her hand off taking the offer. For now, all she could take was her seat off to the left and one row in from the back. Choosing the very last row meant being showered with witless conversation from those who just stopped in for a quick look. Fuck that.

Eliza began to grow impatient. The place of solace that she was seeking was quickly turning to a place of doom and gloom. The group of three in front and the guy on the end (that might have been the projectionist for all she knew) were slowly becoming symbols of her tragedy. The two guys and one girl were easily Ryan, Jesse and Lily, waiting for her to return from her third bathroom break in an hour. The guy alone to her right staring blankly forward was any number of things: her, her life, her future – maybe death waiting her out. Why the hell didn't they start the fucking movie, she wondered. It had to be one-fifteen by now. She thought of how there were at least five more showings after this one and could see absolutely no reason why they should wait one more second. Waiting like this was wrong. It was disrespectful, actually. Who the hell did they think they—

The screen suddenly turned black, and an unidentifiable hum emitted from no fewer than five places around the room. Then came that familiar Warner Brothers logo floating proudly in a blue sky dappled by fluffy clouds. Seconds later, total black took over the screen and she could hear the steady heartbeat of drums and a lone, moaning keyboard. The opening tune was one of her favorites. The salient, soaring main vocal answered by the children's choir told her to:

Cry little sister (thou shall not fall)
Come to your brother, (thou shall not die)
Unchain me sister, (thou shall not fear)
Love is with your brother, (thou shall not kill)

She wanted to go to him, them. She wanted to stop falling. She wanted to stop being afraid.

But cry is what she did. The images, the music, seeing the vampire David on the carousel with his crew; it all reminded her of Ryan. They had always loved this movie, and it awoke in them an affinity for that decade of popular culture. The way many young couples talked about how they wished they were back in medieval England romancing one another on the back of a horse, that's how she and Ryan had felt about the 80's and the back of a carousel horse. And it wasn't just this movie that sold them; it was the music, too. She even used to wear day-glow bracelets and super wide belts and do Ryan's hair up in a blonde spiked mullet just like David. It didn't even matter that his goatee wasn't coming in quite right. It was all about the long black jacket, the walk and the attitude. He did a perfect David. It was all so perfect.

Eliza began to sob, which threw her at first since she didn't think she had many tears left. And while some doctor that she could never afford would probably tell her it was a good sign and that she was on her way to healing, inside she knew that was wrong. Her tears were not tears of acceptance or mourning. In fact, they weren't about Ryan at all. These tears were about her, and an arrangement that she was making with herself about what was to come.

Dmitrije stopped so suddenly in his tracks, his toes pushed up against the front of his chocolate brown oxfords. He wasn't sure if he was more like a snake reacting to subtle vibrations on the ground, or a vulture with a beak sensitive to the slightest hint of carrion. Either species was considered vile by the majority of the population, but were both to unexpectedly disappear there would be an awful lot of rot to go around. So few thought ahead with any real objectivity, and even fewer bothered to put more than two and two together. Straight lines: that's what everyone wanted. Simple solutions, opposite reactions, swift decisions – one of the reasons he had given up his practice was because he knew there was rarely any such thing. Could he possess within himself the potential to be a cold-blooded killer? He knew it was true. Most of the time he didn't know how he would react in a certain situation until the situation presented itself. In this case, he was searching, not stalking. He sought knowledge, not sustenance.

Eliza's mouth went slack. Some unwanted light was ruining Jason Patrick's reaction after he read what was spray-painted on a billboard that had just greeted he and his family. The front read "Welcome to Santa Carla", but on the back someone had added "The Murder Capital of the World". It was the audience's job to determine what Jason thought about this particularly gloomy portent, only the moment was lost because a "peeker", Eliza assumed, had felt the need to indulge some pointless curiosity and open the door. The temporary bout with repulsion halted her tears, and while it hadn't changed her mind about things – those things – it did make her sigh loudly in protest. She refused to let the peeker think what he or she had done was remotely acceptable. Up to that point she hadn't made up her mind whether she was going to sit through the entire movie, but now she felt like she needed to stick around a little longer.

And it was only getting worse. The peeker had taken a seat right behind her, intent on ruining her moment. She almost wanted to turn around and claw his or her eyes out.

"I hope I didn't make you angry," his voice was cool, calm and familiar. "If I did, I'm sorry."

Eliza spun around to find the old book guy's apologetic expression softly lit by the opening day scene. He said, "I got hung up by some business and wasn't going to get another chance to see this. It's one of my favorites."

She spun back around. "Mine, too."

Dmitrije watched her, concentrating on her aura. He had never seen one so black in someone so young and beautiful. He knew, of course, that it was what had been attracting him. The "black flame" he used to call it. She had been drawing light and energy to herself, and transforming it – *consuming* it. As a result, he had no doubt that she had been repelling people the entire day. Those who weren't designed to destroy light would sense her consumptive power and flee. Most of the time they didn't even realize they were running from her. The subconscious mind uses a variety of techniques when seeking to communicate with it's more easily accessible other half. It might create a problem that required specific work to solve, such as something one must tend to or protect. Other times it will force the conscious to focus on a particular need, even if that need has recently been met such as eating, drinking, or the obtainment of some form of security. These loops can often explain cravings, and in their absence, what has come to be referred to as "free floating anxiety".

Similarly, addiction to drugs is often the result of a failing coping mechanism. One seeks to escape a fear or a force that is directing one's conscious behavior, either mental or physical. Helpless to break the cycle, chemicals are employed to slow down all conscious reactions. The effect is that of running in place in the path of a devitalizing, psychological juggernaut. Again, instant fixes and automatic solutions were the bane to modern, human society. This girl was in harm's way, how specifically he didn't know, but it was evidently clear and metaphysically transparent that she was in danger of consuming every last bit of light around her until there was none. Once that happened, there was but one method of escape.

Dmitrije leaned in close to her ear and said, "I saw your auction...you must be a very trusting person."

He thought he would try opening her up with a simple observation.

Eliza kept her face pointed at the screen and replied, "What a creepy fucking thing to say."

Her whispering did nothing to remove the sting from the sentiment. She was right. It was the wrong place, the wrong time, and the wrong words. But he got her talking.

He leaned in again, but not as close. “I’m sorry, Eliza. What I meant to say was...if it works, I might try the idea myself. With your permission, of course.”

She shrugged. Get the hint – and a mint while you’re at it – buddy. Jumping Jesus on a hand-truck his timing was shit.

“Eliza...I wonder if we might be able to talk.”

“Is it important?” she scolded.

It was an exceptional question, he thought. Were he to answer “yes”, he was clearly insane and possibly dangerous. If he answered “no”, then that would be the end of that. He took another tack.

“I’m afraid it could be...in fact, I have the feeling I might be too late.” What an unusual sensation it was for him to be acting without a full understanding as to what his motives were. It was as if he was using his hunting skills to heal rather than destroy, and he wondered if the man he was and the one he used to be had struck up some kind of an agreement. If not, even if something was coming undone, he couldn’t resist the urge to keep pulling at it.

Eliza couldn’t respond. She thought she needed to, but it was hopeless. The condition of his being correct yet still unknowing froze her response mechanisms. She continued to watch the screen, but the words that were coming out of the actors’ mouths had no meaning at all. Should she get up and walk out? What kind of signal would that send? Maybe she should she just listen to what he had to say? What did he mean he was “too late?” Old Eliza would have stood up, told him off right then and there, and reported his high profile ass to the hotel manager. New Eliza, however, knew two things Old Eliza did not: one, he wouldn’t have approached Old Eliza for reasons she may want to know, and two, she had nothing left to lose.

“Outside.” She wasn’t giving an order, but rather answering an unasked question. Then she stood up, and without looking at him, eclipsed the projection on her way out.

Dmitrije stepped into the mezzanine floor hall where Eliza was waiting for him: arms crossed and eyes blinking as if signaling in Morse code to spit out whatever he had to say.

"I hope I didn't startle you," he began. "It wasn't my intention."

She got mad. "What was your intention, then? Are you a pervert or something? Might as well be up front about it...you wouldn't be the first."

"No, it's nothing like that," he replied. "Would you like to take a walk?

"A walk? Where?" She wasn't grateful enough for his interrupting her darkest moment to just trod off anywhere with him.

"I know a place," he said, softly. "We'll be in plain site. I promise."

The Wyndorf was famous for its family recreation facilities. They were located in the rear of the hotel on the first floor, far away from convention activity. There was a large game room, a gym with a small basketball court, and an indoor/outdoor pool area with a retractable tinted roof. Because the weather had been unpredictable lately, there were only a few kids playing in its waters in full view of a mother who wouldn't have lasted five minutes in the open sun without her fair skin exploding. Dmitrije and Eliza entered the pool area through a glass, automatic sliding door that swallowed up any trailing convention noise as it closed behind them.

Eliza felt herself relax in the idle environment. A small fountain percolated tranquilly to her right near a collection of tables and chairs that were elegantly crafted from what she thought was iron of some sort. They looked antique, something she could see decorating a patio of her own with, and she found herself wanting to try one of them out.

Dmitrije seemed to read her thoughts. "Shall we have a seat?"

"Sure."

They walked, several steps apart, both of them relieved by the way the fountain and the chitchat of the young boys kept the scene from falling into an awkward silence.

Dmitrije gestured to a chair near – but not too near – the one he had claimed for himself and waited for her to sit. Eliza slid into it and immediately hiked her feet up on the seat so that her knees provided ample cover for her heart. She was guarded, that much he expected. What he hadn't foreseen was how little she would fear him. Taking one's feet off of terra firma was a choice made by only the most confident of patients. It meant their flight response was inactive. Not that she was a patient, of course. He didn't know what she was, other then someone who he needed to get to know.

"Thank you for agreeing to this," he said, putting his arms on the table so she could see them. It was another subtle trick to gain trust.

"It's nice out here…I feel better," said Eliza. "Maybe I should thank *you*."

"Not necessary. I would like to ask you a question, however…if that would be alright." He absently swept a small amount of dirt from the surface of the table.

"Yeah, sure," she answered. "Shoot."

"Am I right in assuming that you were extremely upset when I found you…in the theater, I mean. I got the sense that you'd been crying." He planned to keep it light, but there was no need to engage in small talk.

"What tipped you off, the wet eyes or the heaving sobs?" She shouldn't have gone there, so she added, "Sorry…I've had an epic fail of a year."

"It's quite alright," he assured her. "No need to apologize. I've had quite the year, myself."

"You look okay to me."

"Do I?"

"Uh-huh. Business seems to be good, anyway."

Her words intrigued him. "Is that what was upsetting you? Business not being so good?"

She guffawed obnoxiously at the suggestion. Like she gave a hairy rat's ass if she never made another penny in her life if it meant she could have Ryan back.

"No, not at all." She inhaled deeply, and let it out saying, "*Whew*…not at all."

He detected a rasp in her voice. "Would you like something to drink? I should have asked."

"No…I'm fine. I mean, I'm not fine but I don't think I could ingest anything right now." She was sure she was sweating. Her armpits felt like they were melting her knees.

"Eliza...before we go on I should probably tell you that I'm not trying to get you to say anything you don't want to say. Your life and what has happened in the past year is yours to protect." He was in full therapist mode now, and it annoyed him. Why can't he just talk like a normal person? He was one for eighty-percent of his life.

"Then what are you trying to get me to say, " she volleyed, "or are you just being nice? Cause if you're just being nice, that's fine. We can be nice for a little bit, if that's what floats your boat. But if you're trying to cure me or some shit like that, then you should know that I'm pretty fucking incurable. I know you're a doctor...I don't know what kind...so maybe old habits are kicking in. Either that or—"

He watched as she bit her tongue. She was right, old habits were kicking in. But had they kicked in all the way, he would have allowed the silence to remain. It was the job of the therapist to constantly call their hand and push the play back to the patient, passively forcing them to tip their hand in return. But he realized at that moment that he wasn't there just to help her help herself. He had needs, too, and he had better stop her because he knew where she was going.

"Or what, Eliza? Do you think I see you as a new character? I don't, you know. To be perfectly honest, I don't know why I'm asking you these questions. I only know that I feel I must." He lowered his eyes and leaned back into his chair, opening up the neutral space between them.

Call.

"Look," her eyes searched the skies, "I'm probably not the best person to talk to right now. And I'm not really in the market to make friends. Fuck...I can't even stand the thought of being anything to anyone right now."

She made a pained face.

Dmitrije's hand flew straight to his mouth, and for a few seconds his entire view became bathed in red. It probably looked to her as if he were reacting in sympathy to her brief moment of intense discomfort. He hoped, anyway. Now wasn't the time to explain what was going on in his upper canines.

"Are you hurt?" he asked, but he already knew. He just needed to know more.

"It's my neck, " she used a rubbing motion with her hand to point out where exactly, "I broke it about six months ago."

"Dear gods...how on earth did you do that?" There were no scars on her face that he could tell, so he ruled out car accident.

"Well, I didn't actually do it. Someone else did. Three someone elses, to be exact." She dug her hands into the pockets of her hoodie, and there was the distinct sound of keys being fondled. "Doctor...um, I'm sorry, I forgot your name."

"Doctor Radan. But please call me Dmitrije."

"Maybe. Doctor, I may have to go do something in a few minutes. I'm telling you because I don't want you to think I'm being rude if I just leave."

"Yes, of course. Is there anything I can do to help?"

"I don't think so. It should only take a couple minutes." She had started to rock a little in her chair. If he was half the doctor he appeared, he probably knew a junkie when he saw one so there was no need to be overly self-conscious.

Dmitrije checked his watch. "I'll tell you what...it's exactly one thirty-seven. Why don't you go and do whatever it is you need to do, I'll check in on a few things, and if you like we can meet back here when you're finished. Say, two o'clock?"

She shrugged, causing another constellation of stars to cloud her vision. She could feel her hip again, too. "Okay," she said through clenched teeth, "I'll check back here in a bit."

"Fine," he said, as he stood out of politeness, "I appreciate your time, I really do." He was no closer to unlocking her secrets, and he wondered how long he would need. Was one day enough? The thought of leaving the hotel and not getting the information he needed made him acutely anxious.

Eliza slinked off her chair and slowly straightened. "No problem," she said emptily, "I guess I'll see you."

He sat back down and watched her walk towards the sliding glass doors. With each step, her purposeful gait degenerated into a pronounced limp. When she arrived at the doors, they zipped open but she didn't pass through. She just stood there looking into the hotel, arms at her sides. It appeared as if she had begun to shake. She turned back towards him, and he rose again from his chair.

"Eliza?" His voice crumbled slightly with concern. He could

see tears in her eyes, and a few fell straight down onto the slate tiles of the patio floor, barely kissing her cheekbones along the way.

"Maybe you'd better come with me," she quivered, "cause if I go and do this thing I need to do...I don't know if I'm coming back."

Saturday

part two

Dmitrije waited outside Eliza's car, observing the traffic on the street in front of the hotel. The Wyndorf was located in a hotel park of sorts, so the street was merely a glorified driveway to all the hotels in the complex with a light at the end of it that let out onto the main highway. A large, covered garage offered free parking across the street from a public bus stop and he figured that most of the cars in it were of non-guests who took advantage of the bus route into the nearby amusements. He was sure this transportation loophole would be rectified once the hotel realized that the full lot was hurting business more than helping it and instated a ticket system.

Some things were easy to fix – when you wanted to fix them, that is. Other matters weren't so easy to adjust no matter how badly they needed it. Case in point: this young girl in the car beside him. He couldn't see in through the reflection of the window too well, but he thought he had seen her swallow at least six, tiny white pills and wash them down with an energy drink of some kind. Tolerance buildup, he thought, generally meant that the method of pain management was incorrect, or addiction had set in. Earlier, he had noticed her become jittery at the incidence of some acute discomfort. He couldn't determine whether it was attributable to physical pain, emotional pain, or some combination of the two. Whichever it was, there could only be one of two reasons why she had just swallowed six pills:

she was on the wrong medication, or there was no medication for what was really wrong with her. He guessed the latter, and gently knocked on the window. Eliza gave him the "thumbs-up" sign. Seconds later, the sound of a door handle alerted Dmitrije to step back.

Eliza climbed out of the car, squinting. The October sun was relentless, and it shone directly onto her face as it worked its way up from the horizon.

"Thanks for waiting," she said with a barely discernable layer of enterprise. "I should be good for another few hours or so."

"Another few hours, eh? Then what…if you don't mind me asking?" He tried his best not to sound remonstrative.

"I don't know."

"May I make a suggestion?"

"What I mean is, I don't know if I mind you asking. Dr Radan, you have to understand something. I wasn't always like this."

"Like what, Eliza?"

Her mind made a round in her stomach like a night nurse listening for the slightest of sounds. Most of the patients would be asleep, but some would have lost their regular pattern of consciousness. For them, night was day and day was a noisy, disruptive, and overly bright night.

She finally found her word.

"Broken."

They took the walk back to the hotel, taking special care not to get run over by the circling cars that were desperately seeking parking spaces. Managing to weave in and out of a crowd of smokers successfully, they passed through the entrance and into an explosion of activity. For her, the commotion was much easier to emotionally accommodate now that she knew help was on the way, and the midday hour meant less of a privacy issue for him. Dmitrije hadn't been to his table since just past noon, and he assumed that anyone who might have approached him in the lobby was now waiting in line and wondering where the hell he was. Together, they stood an arm and a half's length apart until someone cut between them on their way out for a cig. At that, Dmitrije closed the gap by a step.

"I suppose I should return to my table. Will you be alright?"

He weighed the possibility of there being an acceptable amount of truth in her answer and came up with fifty percent.

"I'll be fine, now," she answered with a sigh. "I'm not that worried about my auction. It'll work or it won't. I'm ready to deal with either outcome."

She sounded to him as if she believed herself, which would have to be good enough. "Very good," he answered with some cheer, "I'll meet you at the pool in, say, ten minutes?"

Eliza rebounded, "You know you don't have to blow off your fans for me."

"By my count I saw most of them last night," he assured her. "And there's always tomorrow, yes?" He could see she needed more information to put the matter at rest. "Eliza...this is as much for me as it is for you."

"Why? You don't even know what's wrong with me. I could be some garden-variety pill junkie with stupid daddy issues for all you know."

"I think there's possibly more to it than that."

"Maybe," she confessed. "Still...what do *you* get out of it?"

"Would it scare you if I told you I wasn't sure?" he replied. It certainly scared him.

"No...I guess not." She didn't really mean it. It was obvious he wanted to get close to her and there were only a few reasons for a stranger to want such a thing. Even if a part of him was acting on some inherent, "doctorly" instinct, she hadn't trusted anyone, not even her own father, since the attack – except maybe Francis and Wendy, but that was for simple things like a shower and an ersatz drink invitation – so why should she trust him?

"Don't let me hold you up any more," she said, digging her hands deeper into her hoodie pockets. "I'll be there. I promise."

He could tell she still hadn't made up her mind. Due in part to his gentle tack, the opportunity to make her feel truly obligated had come and gone. He hadn't exactly saved her life, or anything. He merely stood by the car – an act that wasn't without some degree of risk – and gave her the responsibility to think twice out of consideration. Apparently, this little half-agreement was her repayment. Fair enough.

"Good. Well...here I go," he reported, freeing her to her neurotic whims. With a mannered grin, he ducked back into the fray.

Eliza stood and watched him. There went another one, walking away. Only this one hadn't wanted to go at all. A part of her was glad he was gone, and, if she was being honest, a part of her wasn't. She could easily end up back in the movie room again, sobbing over Ryan and declaring a fate that, with assent, brought with it a horrifying numbness. Speaking of numbness, she didn't dare test her neck yet, but her hip still hurt. So while she was waiting for the "cool rag on her forehead" she thought she might wade into an open section of the lobby, hug a wall, and wait for the pain to go away.

On her way she passed the Celeb Room and she could hear the myriad of murmurs all mixing together in a grand cacophony of kiss-ass. Dr. Radan didn't need to scare up any love of his own, but he did spook her a little. Doctors always did, so maybe one following her around was what had her at such penetrating unease. His eyes were too intelligent to be considered simply "kind", and even if he was acting on some do-gooder need, his voice made her feel dangerously drowsy. Eliza knew she was in a psychological crisis when the very thought of relaxation and comfort without the help of pills registered to her as a warning sign. Just how long could she live alternately in a hole and on-guard, with the blur of opiates tenuously holding it all together? Wandering around the one place that used to feel like her planet and now felt like any other planet in the solar system made her wonder if zombies knew they were zombies. At what point when they turn do they know what they are? Do they spend a little time sorting out some existential conflict, or do they operate out of pure instinct? Someone there had to know. Who could she ask?

At that moment she turned to look into the Celeb Room and what she saw made her take a beeline into the hive.

Celeb Rooms came with an enforced order that made them easy to swim through. Lines to the various stars held fast to their structure, and rarely if ever did someone bail because they lost patience. Due to the relatively small size of the room and the rather large amount of celebrities in attendance, the lines tended to double back, with a few twisting in odd directions that reminded her of a frozen conga line. It forced Eliza to plan out her routes a little more carefully than usual, but once she saw the person she wanted to get to, she realized reaching him wouldn't be much of a task at all. He only had about five people waiting to squeeze his disgustingly large biceps, whereas the person whose attention she really wanted to win would set her back an hour and a half at least. This wasn't going to be easy, but just like everything else she did since arriving yesterday afternoon, she would have to ignore the accompanying unpleasantness and plow forward.

She got in line just as the person in the front, a man who was probably in his late twenties and on his own cycle of the juice, shook Dane Harding's hand and walked away with his autographed picture. This made her fifth now, and she wondered if she would have to cough up twenty bucks for one of Dane's horrible press photos. If she didn't, it might be too awkward trying to convince him she gave a shit about his lame career. If she had to, she would, but she would make sure she grabbed a picture of him that showed as little of his face behind the camouflage makeup as possible.

She could see Lorena listening intently to a woman with hair extensions hanging all the way down to her ass. The woman was saying something about a pet shelter, Eliza thought she heard, and Lorena was being thoughtful enough to wave her freshly signed photo back and forth to help the ink dry. This must have delighted the woman, as it bought her a few extra seconds to chat. On the other hand, it must have annoyed everyone else in line because of the exact same reason.

A five-second flirtation between Lorena and Dane brought on a wave of nausea in Eliza's stomach as both had just said goodbye to a fan at the same time and took the simultaneous lull as an opportunity to swap gushes. Eliza had to ask herself if she was jealous. The look on her face probably gave her away, but had someone noticed, they would have gotten the story all wrong. She wasn't sexually attracted to either of them, really, but that didn't stop her from adopting a jilted stance to the sight of Lorena blushing over something completely stupid Dane Harding had probably said.

The next three boys were together and the whole episode went quickly. It looked like they all had to pee or something. So she stepped up to the table and perused the photos. There was one that was actually a screenshot from *Landmine 9: Limb from*

Limb. And much to her surprise, there was a dark-haired Lorena in it. She was screaming and attempting to block a bayonet attack. She would be unsuccessful, Eliza recalled. And Corporal Punishment would do to her what he did to all of his victims after he had wounded them to the point where they couldn't move: place a grenade in their hands and walk away, allowing them to choose when they wanted their suffering to end. Some died before choosing, thus releasing the pin posthumously. Others tried to throw it at him, but never could quite get it to travel the distance required to end their assailant's reign of terror, or, sadly, Dane's acting career. But at least now she thought she knew what the flirtation she had witnessed might have been about. They had done a movie together, after all, and Eliza simply didn't realize the soap star had been in *L9:LfL* because of her hair color. Maybe, she sorely hoped, Lorena only sounded excited about him earlier because she thought it would cheer up her pukey little acquaintance. There may be no hope for Lorena's fortune telling future, but there was still some yet for her romantic one.

The boy in front of her took his signed DVD from Dane, handed him three crisp tens, and walked away without shaking his hand. It was her turn.

Dane looked up at her with eyes as dead and glassy as the ones they were selling outside for three bucks a pair.

"Howdy," he bellowed. "Whatcha got there?"

He reminded Eliza of someone that she couldn't place but understood to be extremely stupid. She looked down and saw that she had picked up the photo of he and Lorena. She didn't even remember doing it. She was probably too busy trying to catch Lorena looking in her direction.

"This," answered Eliza, as she dropped the photo in front of him with all the enthusiasm of a child about to receive a throat swab.

"What would you like it to say?" asked Dane, with a cock of an eyebrow.

He wasn't being a jerk, Eliza thought, but he was irritating her. *Put anything down, asshole. Can't you see I'm here for Lorena?*

"To Maddie...a beautiful girl and my biggest fan," she recited. "with love...and whatever." She thought that would take the imbecile long enough.

Lorena, she noticed, hadn't so much as glanced in her direction. She would have to go to plan B.

"So, Dane," Eliza started, "do you think that zombies know that they're zombies?"

She saw that Dane was on the "biggest fan" part of her inscription, and stopped mid-letter. He seemed to relish the chance to impart some wisdom on the subject.

"Do zombies know they're zombies," he repeated, like it was a question of such deep complexity that only a long evening with several bottles of wine would be sufficient enough to address it. "Hmm...that's a good one. "

He leaned back as if to see the big picture more clearly, and then leaned to his right. "Isn't that a good one, Lorena?" he shouted.

Lorena was smiling and taking a photo from someone in expertly applied werewolf facial hair – at least Eliza *thought* it was applied – who wanted her to write "something sexy" on it.

"One sec," she said, and continued writing. She handed the photo back, content that the beast's savagery was effectively soothed by what she had made up on the spot. She turned to Dane and asked, "What's this now?"

Eliza made her move.

"Do zombies know they're zombies?" she interjected, cutting Dane off. "If they do, wouldn't that mean that at some point they were aware of being turned? And if they don't kill themselves...if they eat and try to survive...does that mean they're cool with it?"

She watched Lorena open her mouth and check Dane for confirmation that the question pertained to her specific field of study. Then she said something brilliant.

"Well, they know other zombies are zombies, don't they?" She was right. If they could tell the difference, and they clearly could, they were probably not just acting on some pure, carnivorous instinct but had at least a basic idea of what it was to be undead.

"Then there was that one," Lorena continued, "what's his name...he shot at that guy near the end."

"Bub," offered Eliza, "from *Day of the Dead*."

This was going well, she thought, even if she was pontificating a little. Fans waiting in Lorena's line were watching them now. They had an audience. People would now know that she and Lorena were friendly. This was better than pills.

"That's him!" said Lorena. She turned and beamed at Dane. "Make sure you make hers out nice. What's her name?"

Eliza felt a bubble form in the back of her throat. Did she just ask him what her name was?

Dane held up the photo and showed Lorena. "Her name's Maddie, see? Can't you read?" He was being playful, and to Eliza's sheer horror, managing to come off "cute" in the process.

"You make sure he gives you a big kiss on there, Maddie," Lorena ordered. Then she switched her attention back to her next customer. "Sorry to keep you waiting," she said. "We had a crisis."

Lorena finished it off with a trained laugh that shook her breasts. What's worse, a quick, soapy look back to Dane told Eliza that the deal was sealed. Unable to move now, she watched in horror as he added "Kisses" and a few "X's and O's" to the bottom of the bogus message, and handed her the photo. It was beyond appalling, now. Not only was it an unmistakable fact that Lorena had forgotten her, but Eliza had actually made it possible for Dane Harding to use her as a foil for his lascivious devices. Being relegated from "Dealer" – which was bad enough – to "Dane Harding Fan" wasn't even the final, humiliating touch. She had actually lost her name.

This zombie definitely knew it was dead.

Dmitrije signed the word "Cough!" and then, "Doctor Dark". It was all that the middle-aged, biker-looking guy wanted. As crude as it was, it worked a small laugh out of him. "You're all that and a rack of ribs," the guy had told him upon receiving his request. It was a compliment, apparently.

A look down the line worried him. When he'd arrived, the queue was no more than a dozen people. They were all extremely polite and understanding of his being missing in action, and it had looked like he would make his pool appointment with time to spare. What he had failed to account for were those who had become fed up with waiting and left, but returned when they saw the line had started moving. There was no way he could excuse himself early now, and he resigned himself to the fact that he would never make it on time unless there was a fire.

She had asked him, in so many words, what he was hoping to gain from their meeting. He really wanted to find an answer for her in order to move past that barrier to their exchange, and he thought he had it. So often lately he had looked at life as a series of things to do. Now, there existed in its overlapping folds something that resembled a purpose. He hadn't clearly defined that purpose, but he was sure it wasn't simply about helping her. Eliza had spoken to him without knowing it, and what she had said had awakened things buried deep inside. The sensation spinning in his head was one of nostalgia and urgency; contradicting notions that could only be compared to a sense of déjà vu that was continuously present under the surface. Like teething for a baby, there existed an irresistible pain that couldn't be left alone. Teething – what an odd thing to consider. Why had he used that metaphor?

Then it hit him. He was wiping a thin layer of dust from the cover of one of his books before handing it back to an adult woman in braces when suddenly it felt as if his mouth had erupted into flames. He responded with a guttural vocalization that he barely recognized to be his own and leapt to his feet, knocking over his chair. The person next in line, a twenty-something boy with red hair and a backwards baseball cap had reacted by emitting a high-pitch squeal and dropping his bag. That started an instantaneous chain reaction that saw more bags dropped and more high-pitched squeals. The guards made a move to separate him from the line, but it wasn't necessary. Most of those who were waiting had backed away, hitting into passersby who in turn slammed into tables of merchandise. Dmitrije didn't care. His mouth was throbbing, and a metallic taste had filled it along with an overproduction of saliva. He didn't know what was happening, but he had to get the hell out of there and fast.

He outstretched one hand to the guard and the other to the people in the aisle in an unspoken offering of peace. Then all he could think to do was raise a finger as if to say, "one minute, please". He would have said as much, but he was afraid to part his lips. If he did, he knew there would be an emanation of drool straight down the front of his shirt that could have filled a coffee cup, and enough had already happened to be embarrassed about. However, his disconsolation was soon displaced by an overpowering fear, forcing him out from behind his table and into a rush for the door. Before he knew it, he was in the hall and running.

He knew where he was going, where he *had* to go. Each step reaffirmed his conclusions as each brought more and more pain to his mouth. There had been a time so long ago when he had suffered a similar attack, but then, things were different. He had felt an abundance of pain and fear, been acutely aware of it to the point where it had taken on hues and smells that he could identify but never explain, only he hadn't shared it. Now, as he pushed passed confused onlookers, stiffening them with shock, he did. Something was wrong. Something was *very* wrong. His connection to it continued to elude him, but there was no denying that this terrible tether was real. Rarely does a species of any kind run towards pain and fear unless they are protecting their young. He had never fathered a child, that much he knew. He also had the persistent suspicion, born of instincts both naturally instilled and artificially acquired, that the bond bedeviling him now was much fiercer.

He hadn't bothered with the elevator, as the entrance to the pool was only one floor down. It could have been considered in the basement had the hotel not been built on the top of a small, meticulously manicured hill of grass. Being where it was allowed for a recreational area to be dug into the side of the mound and voluntarily exposed to the elements. He had initially thought of running out the front of the lobby and around the entire building so that fewer people would be witness to his hysteria. Thinking better of it, he took the stairs where only a single member of housekeeping would be found, peeking over an armful of fresh towels.

He arrived at the sliding glass doors which opened a touch too slowly for his liking, causing him to turn sideways to make it through. The mother and her charges had left, leaving a few water stains to mark their exit. It was eerily quiet. Only the bubbling of the fountain could be heard, which made him nervous in a new way. Had he picked the wrong place to try and find her? The pain told him different. It had traveled along a network of nerves, spreading out over his entire face. His jaw hurt, probably from clenching it. A scowl had begun to give him a headache.

The pool. How could he not have thought of the pool? He dashed to the edge of it, and scanned the softly undulating surface. He couldn't see anything; at least he thought he couldn't. The tinted roof cast the entire reflective area in a dusky brown, but as far as he could tell there were no anomalies in the pattern. Then he noticed that he was looking in the shallow end. He ran the length of the pool, observing the depth markers that had been painted on the side: 5ft, 6ft, 7ft – all the way to 10ft. When he got to the diving board, he used it to support himself so he could lean out and lower his eyes closer to the surface. His face was burning so badly he nearly let it dip under.

No, it couldn't be.

With a splash, he was heading towards the bottom. He hadn't even taken an extra breath.

Saturday

part three

There are moments in one's life that irrefutably define who one is as a member of society. They have nothing to do with promotions, degrees, or selections from one of life's many menus. They are moments that are often only experienced in retrospect, as they happen too fast for most brains to process. They are the moments that hold life and death with a cold, closed fist – with fingers that wait to be pried open by one's very soul. Dmitrije contemplated this truth as he sat in his robe in a chair by the window in his room, and looked into an indifferent sky through a tiny sliver between the curtains. It was still blue, he noticed, as blue as the unoxygenated blood in his veins. Nothing that had happened today, yesterday or tomorrow would ever change what color the sky wanted to be. Had what happened changed him? Had it defined him, or more accurately, *re*-defined him? Had it told him anything at all?

He turned away from the window and looked at the girl on the bed. Her color, no longer sky blue, had taken on complimentary shades of faded olive and blushing pink over the last half an hour. Her breathing was still a little shallow, but her pulse was strong. He borrowed the sky's disposition and examined her with a distant professionalism. Despite her increased tolerance, it couldn't be overstated how lucky she was with all those pills – oxycodone from the looks of them – in her system. They could have easily relaxed her laryngospasm, or constriction of the larynx. Had she "wet drowned", her lungs would have filled with fluid and even though she may have been resuscitated she would have still been in grave danger from lung collapse or edema. He had no idea how long she had been unconscious, but he guessed around two to three minutes from the time he felt the pain in his mouth to the time he brought her around. Six minutes would have meant stone death. Had he been in his room when it happened and been forced to take the elevator – he didn't want to think about it. He had seen too many die in a former lifetime and it didn't do him any good to bring those memories into this one. Better to just accept that she would awaken with little more than a headache and the same old problems that brought it on.

Eliza stirred a bit, and coughed. She opened her eyes and Dimitrije could tell that she had no idea where she was.

"Eliza...it's me. Dr. Radan." He had noticed before that she still didn't call him by his first name. "Doctor" might be more appropriate at the moment, anyway. "How do you feel?"

"Like such a fucking idiot."

"Now don't get excited," he said, as if slipping into an old pair of shoes. "Everything is fine."

He rose from the chair and took a seat next to her on the bed. She was crying.

"I want you to look here." He turned on a penlight and brought it over her face. "Please."

She did, and he reached over to pull her teary eyelid open a tad wider. She was still high, but she seemed alert. Luckily, he was able to get her to his room without too many people seeing. She was able to support herself a little so she just appeared drunk, which wouldn't have surprised anyone. If they weren't concerned that there were no lifeguards on duty (they so rarely are in Florida, he noticed) they wouldn't have looked twice at an older man assisting his daughter into the elevator. He had the good sense to remove his shirt and wrap both of them in a towel so as too appear returning from a swim. Once he got her to his room, he made the decision to evaluate her himself, sparing her a litany of inquiries from various authorities. Yes, he was sure this was the reason, save one selfish one.

"You...saved me," she whispered, lower lip trembling. "Why?"

"Are you disappointed?" he asked.

Now that she was awake and alert, he had to determine the likelihood of having to save her again. He was, he remembered, on the 18th floor.

"I don't know," she whimpered. "Thanks and everything... but I was in there for a reason."

Dmitrije flashed a look of disappointment. "Rather rude, don't you think?"

"Why?" she asked.

She was definitely in a bad way. People who really want to die, he found, come to a point where they see it like any other decision one makes in life: buy the paper; have a brandy; choose a profession; kill yourself – they all held equal weight. He would have to nudge the fulcrum of the conversation a few inches off center if he was to get anywhere.

"Well," he countered, "you promised to meet me there, didn't you?"

"I was there, wasn't I?" she responded

That was a sneaky backhand, thought Dmitrije. He followed with, "Yes, but you hadn't let on that it was something you might do."

"Yes, I did."

Of course, she was right. Now he would have to change the direction of the conversation altogether.

"Eliza, since you're so determined not to be, I wonder if you would give me the honor of knowing why."

"You mean before I do it again?" Things had gotten easier since she already died once, so there was little need to be subtle.

"Yes. Before you do it again." His only move was to call her bluff. "I think I've earned an explanation, don't you?"

"Maybe."

"Then please," he said, getting to his feet and walking back to his chair, "Whenever you're ready."

Eliza sat up on the bed and crossed her legs, which made her laugh because she did it without crying out in agony.

"I guess I should start at the beginning," she said.

"That sounds like a wonderful idea." He would keep it light if she insisted.

"My soul mate is dead, my body hurts from head to toe, and

I hate my father," she said, matter-of-factly. "Well, I can't say I *hate* him, I guess...any more than a shoe hates the person wearing it."

"He wears you down, " he offered with a cross of his legs.

"More like *they* wear *him* down," she offered, correcting him. "Personally, I think what happened to me is too much for him and his new family to handle. He probably blames himself a little, so if dealing with me means dealing with it, then birthday cards and short phone calls will have to do. Don't get me wrong, I'm not the easiest person to sit down and have a good cry with and I can't just go shop it off...we're just really different." She grabbed a pillow and plopped it on her lap. "And that's pretty much it."

Dmitrije sat perfectly still and examined her face. That was it as far as she was concerned, but there were enormous holes in her biography.

"Eliza, if I may ask...do your injuries have anything to do with your boyfriend – sorry – your *soul mate's* death?" He was careful not to come off patronizing.

She made a face and said, "Duh."

"I'm guessing it wasn't a car accident, am I right?" He would do this by process of elimination if necessary.

"Actually, we got beat up. And I got raped."

Dmitrije watched Eliza fluff the pillow as if she were talking about a boring day at a carnival.

"At least that's what they told me," she added. "I barely remember anything. The paramedics said they found me holding Ryan's head on my lap, and that my leg was twisted out all funny. They said I was screaming for help. I don't know how you can forget stuff like that, but I did. The police gave me these mug shots to go through but they all looked the same to me. On the stand, they ripped me to pieces on account of my amnesia. Two of the guys had cuts and bruises on their hands and had been spotted in the area at the time of the attack but it wasn't enough, they said. Kind of fucked up."

Dmitrije felt a twinge on his gums. What astonished him was how little of a twinge it was. Here this young girl was recounting a horrific incident, the source of unbearable pain that had helped put her at the bottom of a pool, and she had almost totally switched off. It was more than a simple case of amnesia. He had seen it before in refugees who were starving and full of disease. There was a resignation that deadened the part of the brain that could reasonably assess the horror of their reality. Even their physical pain had been replaced by a phantom comfort of sorts. He had seen young children crawl off and simply stop breathing as if by choice. He had witnessed mothers slitting their own throats over the lifeless, little corpses with no more than a twist of their mouths.

"Eliza, do you know what hypnotherapy is?" asked Dmitrije.

"Kind of," she answered, her inflection almost childlike.

"Hypnotherapy is used for many things – things you might find interesting – like pain management, and what we call hypnoanalysis, which therapists use to help clients recall events of their past so that they don't control their lives."

"But I know what happened to me. And no offense or anything, but that pain stuff sounds like a crock." Her hip started to hurt, so she swung her leg out over the edge of the bed.

"It doesn't work for everyone, no. But for some it's given them a new lease on life." He sounded like a cable commercial so he needed to keep going before he lost her. "Eliza, understanding the basic details of something traumatic that has happened to you is much different than really knowing them, isn't it?"

Eliza drove a fist into the pillow, and said, "Okay, but what's your point?"

Dmitrije was encouraged by her show of emotion.

"I'd like to put you under, if you'll give me permission," he said. "You won't remember a thing if you don't want to, but it would help me immensely to understand what you're going through."

He watched her eyes blink rapidly as if to filter the information he was giving her in order to better absorb it.

"What do you say?" he asked.

He watched her right index finger dig into the pillow on her lap and waited anxiously for her to strike a small vein of hope.

She finally looked up and said, "Okay…I'm only asking this hypothetically cause I'm really past the point of caring."

"Yes, of course," said Dimitrije. "Go on."

"If I remember all this stuff like you're saying, what would I have to do then?"

He leaned forward, resting his elbows on his knees. He wanted to look as unassuming as he could.

"Whatever you wanted to do," he answered.

"What if I want to do nothing?" she replied, stripping the situation down to its bare bones.

He thought for a second, and while straightening his back, said, "When you've tried everything, Eliza...all you have left is nothing."

Nonsense makes sense sometimes, especially to those who have tried to kill themselves. It had to be the reason Eliza agreed to lay back on the bed and focus on the hole patterns in the ceiling. The Wyndorf had selected one-foot by one-foot tiles to hang above the heads of their guests, which were textured with pinholes for reasons that he believed he would never know for sure. Certainly it wasn't to assist in making someone relaxed, suggestible and drowsy, although he was willing to bet he was close.

He had asked her some rudimentary questions so that he might better set the stage. He would try an affect bridge – a technique where the hypnotherapist associates a patient's hidden memories with an emotional state – in order to recover her ordeal. Any sounds or images she could remember would help take her back to the point of the attack more easily. She knew, along with anyone who read the newspaper, where it had happened and what the weather was like on that day. And he already knew who was with her. After she shared a few more details about the area, he felt it was time to get to the dark heart of the matter.

As she continued to focus, he asked her politely to close her eyes and sleep, and she did. Years ago, hypnotists would swing a watch so that after twenty or thirty minutes the eyes would become tired. How thrilling it must have been for the first hypnotist to discover that you simply had to ask a patient to respond in the way you wanted. In this case, the conditions for a successful induction through such suggestions were set: he had established authority, she was immobile in an unusual environment and he could already tell that the mysterious pinholes were doing their job. He might have tried a rapid induction that would put her under in seconds, but that method involved a sudden shock. He had perfected a version that, if someone were heavily fatigued, injured or already in shock, required only a simple touch. For this case, it seemed inappropriate. There had been enough shock for both of them already.

It was time to send her back. He would have to do so carefully. He regretted not buying something to numb his gums. This wasn't going to be pretty.

"Eliza, I want you to picture yourself walking along the estuary a few miles from your apartment. It's the one with the brown pelican that used to scare you but to whom you eventually gave the name...what was it again?"

"Boris," she answered.

"Boris. Very good. He dives into the water from a tree that has been damaged in a storm. Most of its leaves are gone. You know the one, don't you?"

"Yes."

She was there. She could smell the salt water. She could hear Boris grunting, and the soft rustle of tall grass.

"Excellent," said Dmitrije. "It's a beautiful Sarasota afternoon, isn't it? And you're walking barefoot on the wet sand. It feels cool as your toes dig into it."

"It feels like cookie dough," she interjected, "I love cookie dough."

A bizarre correlation, Dmitrije thought, until he gave it a moment. He smiled and continued.

"You're not alone, are you?"

"No. Ryan is here," she giggled. "He's being stupid as usual."

"Oh?" Dmitrije asked.

"Boris doesn't want to be pet, but Ryan keeps trying."

Dmitrije caught himself not wanting to ruin what sounded like the kind of afternoon every girl should be allowed to have, but he had to keep going.

"Eliza, there is someone else there with you and Ryan." He watched as she scowled a bit. It didn't appear to be a scowl of anger or pain, but one of simple curiosity. "Can you see them?"

Eliza looked out across the water and what had been making that buzzing sound had gotten close enough to see. It was one of those swamp boat things with the big fan in the back. It was moving fast. There were maybe three people on it, but she couldn't tell if they were male or female, adults or children.

"I can see them," she said. "They don't see us, though. I think they're going to...oh, no, here they come." She scraped her upper lip with her lower front teeth. "They're coming right at us."

Dmitrije began to feel a little lightheaded. It was almost three o'clock. The events of the day had come to collect their fee. Or was it the men in the boat?

"Can you see them now, Eliza?" he asked.

"Yeah...one of 'em's got binoculars."

"What is Ryan doing?" he inquired with a touch more urgency than he had intended.

"Ryan's walking out," she said nervously. "I'm telling him not to but he's like that. He's stupid."

She was worried. The closer they came the bigger they looked. And there were definitely three of them.

"I don't want him to go out," she said, anxiously.

Dmitrije felt himself get angry. He knew he mustn't become emotionally involved. It wasn't professional. Beyond that, it just wasn't smart. He was being stupid, just like Ryan.

"Ryan's talking to them," she continued. "I don't know what he said but one of 'em stood up and he looks pissed off. Maybe he's lost. I hope he's lost."

She could see Ryan shrugging and raising his arms as if he was telling them he didn't know, he didn't know. She could hear them now. Their voices were louder because they were angry about something. The fat one with the short, dark hair and some kind of chest tattoo looked like he was trying to explain. He was showing him something in his hand – binoculars maybe. Come on, Ryan, she thought. Just turn around and run back. Fuck these assholes.

Ryan looked back at her and when he did one of the skinny ones hit him in the side of the head. Ryan stumbled, but stayed on his feet cause the water was about two feet deep and it held him up just enough. His not falling seemed to piss them off even more, as the other skinny one jumped from the boat and punched him right in the eye. Ryan fell onto his back, and disappeared under the water for a second. Get up, baby...

She screamed.

Dmitrije watched Eliza scream in terror. He watched her body tremble which caused him to brace himself in case he had to stop her from vibrating off the bed. He wanted to stop her, but was it out of the goodness of his heart or because his face was boiling? Whatever the reason, he knew that he couldn't.

At that moment he was overcome with a self-loathing that he hadn't felt since *her*. He was a doctor. No, he hadn't been a doctor in a long time. He stopped when he could no longer handle the helplessness he felt in the shadow of the insurmountable sickness of mankind. So he had decided to help people get medication they couldn't afford until it became all about helping them getting their cocks hard and their minds blandly indifferent. At last, he had pretended to be a doctor in mind alone – an evil one. He had done it easily and without regret. So what was he now?

She stopped screaming with an abrupt choke of tears and pursed her lips tightly. They were so red from the strain that they appeared covered in blood.

"Run, Ryan! Run!" she yelled, her fists bouncing on the mattress with each word.

But he didn't. He was fighting back. It looked for a minute like he wanted to run, but where the water had helped him keep his balance before it was now slowing him down. She needed to get help, but she didn't want to leave him here alone. By the time she found someone, it would be too late. Maybe they would stop soon, she thought. Maybe they would get tired. But they didn't. They kept hitting him, and she could see that his face was swelling badly. He couldn't lie down and cover his head because he was in two feet of water. He had to take it. How much could he take?

She looked at Boris, who had walked down the shoreline a bit as if he didn't want to be bothered and she got angry with him. She was on her own. She thought to grab a rock, but what would she do with it? What good would it do? No, she would have to use her fists, and her feet, and bite.

"Get the fuck away from him," she yelled, anger displacing fear with the flick of a switch, "you redneck motherfuckers!"

Dmitrije looked on in wonder and dismay. She was convulsing now as if striking and being struck. This young girl – one hundred and five pounds soaking wet (and he would know) – had faced her boyfriend's attackers. She was trying to bite. Good for her, he thought. Eliza Lowell had run into the pain and fear, and she had survived. She was a survivor. Yes, she received a brutal beating and had succumbed to unspeakable cruelty, but she had lived. Only, to what end? Did she fight so hard just to wind up at the bottom of a pool?

"He's so heavy," she continued, after having suddenly gone quiet, "even in the water. I've got to get him out of the water." She was hoarse, her voice constricted. "My neck is killing me…I think I lost my left eye. No, I can feel it…I just can't see out of it. Why won't they leave? Ryan, *wake up*."

Dmitrije gripped the armrests of his chair. He wanted to crush them. He wanted to rip them off and throw them into the mirror to destroy his reflection. What was it about his own image that angered him so? He wasn't hurting her. He hadn't done anything to her soul mate. But he had hurt people in the past. He had deceived them, too. He had deceived Eliza.

She stopped fighting, or so it appeared. In fact, she stopped talking completely. There were only faint whispers spilling from her lips, but he couldn't make out what she was saying. Perhaps she was trying to comfort Ryan. Dmitrije knew that he had to keep her going a little more. If he didn't, she might never finish this. He may have been uncertain about who he was and what his intentions were, but he still had complete faith in the science he had studied for so long.

He wiped his brow, took a deep breath, and started in gently, "Eliza, where are you now?"

She shook her head as if to say "no". The scowl she was making was no longer one of curiosity. The deep furrows could only be interpreted as profound disbelief.

He tried again. "Eliza, where are the men. What are they doing?"

"One of them," she said, "is pulling Ryan away from the water… like he doesn't want him to drown. Ryan, look at me…*please*."

But he lay there on the cookie dough and didn't move. He was on his back and his face was to one side where she could see it. It was messed up so bad she could only tell it was him by his blonde hair and skinny arms. At least they had finally left him alone. Now, all she wanted him to do was open his eyes just once and look at her before they started with her again. She wanted to know he was okay but she didn't want him to see them touching her. What if he woke up and they were still doing things? He might say something, or try and fight them again. And then they wouldn't leave him alone anymore. She wanted him to wake up, and at the same time, she didn't.

Then Ryan disappeared. She was sure he was still there but both her eyes were practically swollen shut. That was better, she thought. Better not to see too much. The boy on top of her now was fat and sweaty. He had stayed on the boat looking through his binoculars, she remembered. She couldn't see his face – she could barely see anything – but she could see his ugly chest tattoo. It was poorly done: a skull of some kind, with snakes writhing through its eyes. He would be finished soon, she thought. The snakes would soon have their fill. He was too excited to last very long like the others had. She had been unconscious for most of their turns, so that was good. She couldn't fight them off anyway. Her neck hurt, her arms felt like they were made of stone, and she couldn't feel her legs. She just wanted him to be done so that she could go to Ryan.

Eliza had gone very quiet. Her breathing had receded, as did the scalding inside Dmitrije's mouth. He fought the urge to touch her. He would have to bring her back slowly, using new associations of happiness and goodness, and it didn't feel right doing that.

"Boris is back," Eliza whispered. "He's in the tree."

Now might be a good time, thought Dmitrije. She hadn't gone to Ryan yet, and there was little to be gained by it, he felt. His death, even though she didn't remember it, marked a very real and damaging contribution to her suicidal inclinations. Mourning him properly was something that needed to be done when she was awake. He also felt the personal need to spare her something, and seeing as it held little scientific consequence in stopping it now, that's what he would do.

"Eliza, I want you to concentrate on Boris in that tree and I want you to think about how he looks to you. His brown feathers...his long beak...can you see him?"

"Yes," she replied. "He's looking into the water."

"Does he look like he's going to dive into it?" Dmitrije asked.

"Uh-huh...I think he's hungry."

She never understood why he was always there, at that cove in the estuary. He never seemed to find any fish to eat; not that she saw. Maybe it was the tree, he liked. Or maybe it wasn't fish or the tree that he wanted at all. Maybe it was her and Ryan that he came to see. Maybe he just wanted to be friendly, but he didn't know how.

Dmitrije waited for her breathing to hold slow and steady, and began again with a soothing delivery.

"Eliza, I want you to continue to look at Boris...his brown feathers...his long beak...and when he dives I want you to follow him into the water. When he hits the water, you're going to wake up and feel refreshed and—"

Dmitrije stopped himself. He had to think what he was doing. If he brought her back now, she would feel refreshed for a few moments and then certainly her body would be set ablaze from all the tensing and activity it had suffered while she was under. Perhaps he should try and induce some pain therapy. She seemed very receptive to suggestion, and he was fairly confident that it would work. Then he had another thought: if he bought her enough time to get through the rest of the convention and return home, what of the next day and the day after that? The pain would return and she would surely turn to her pills before she sought out a new doctor, or bothered to try and contact him. Would he have simply managed to relieve himself of duty like he had done with *her?* There were only two other options, both extreme, and both, as far as he knew, very permanent.

He suddenly felt very weak. There was no putting a feeding off any longer. If he did, he wouldn't be alert enough to make the right decision. However, there was still the issue of what he would do after. He would have to go somewhere until he calmed down. There was no telling how he would react after the influence of Eliza's memory recovery. But where would he go? He was in a hotel full of people and many of them knew him. Drawing attention to her now would be even worse. Leaving the grounds was out of the question, as well. Not only did he not want to leave her here by herself in a somnambulistic state, the sun was too bright to risk any prolonged exposure to it. He had no car, and nowhere he knew to go. He could get disoriented, or worse.

Dmitrije withdrew his leather pouch from the refrigerator and after a cursory inspection of Eliza, carried it with him into the bathroom.

Once inside, he locked the door. It would be powerless to hold him if he really wanted out, but at least the act of unlocking it gave him another chance to remember where he was and what was happening. It could mean all the difference to both of them.

He sat on the closed toilet lid and got an idea. He reached into the tub and began running the water. The sound escaping through the door would only help Eliza, he thought, and if someone came in looking for him – again, it bought him time. At the very worst, he could throw his head underneath to maybe jolt himself under control. He hadn't considered these kinds of problems when he made the choice to be this way. Had he thought through every possible scenario, it probably wouldn't have changed his mind anyway.

He opened the pouch, made his selection, and popped the cap. He was very weak now so he didn't waste anytime throwing it back. That might have been a small blunder, as putting it under the tongue assured better absorption into his bloodstream. The thought gave him the idea to have another, and he didn't need to drink the whole thing. A little sublingual succor could help prime things and make them go smoothly. It would mean wasting a vial, but in the circumstances it may be more prudent than wasteful. And there were ways to get more – a syringe method, several of which he always carried with him – if he really had to.

It made sense so he cracked another one, placed a tiny drop under his tongue, and mixed the rest of it into the water slipping down the drain of the tub. He placed the vial along with the first one back into the pouch and closed it. And although he was loath to, he turned his head towards the mirror and looked into his eyes.

“Nothing to do now but wait, Dr. Radan,” he said aloud, hoping that hearing himself addressed by that name would keep the side of his personality he trusted close by.

Saturday

part four

Dr. Radan stood over the supine body of Eliza Lowell, staring. Nearly an hour had past, and he only just felt well enough to leave the confines of the bathroom. As far as he could tell, the yelling and the breaking hadn't disrupted her sleep.

He looked down at his hand. It had been bandaged with one of the smaller towels from the rack. He hadn't remembered doing it, so it must have happened soon after the drop took effect. He hadn't thought of *her*, either. It was the first time in a long time that he hadn't. But there were other matters to attend, and he wanted to stay focused. If that meant to leave Racak behind forever – if it meant to let her spirit rise like a black bird into the grey, Kosovo sky – perhaps that was what he should do.

He could still feel the rage coursing through his veins, and he imagined a handful of jacks slaloming down a drainpipe. No one had heard a thing, and no one had come looking. That was odd. Maybe they did send someone up and, after putting an ear to the door, whomever it was had thought better than to knock or call security. Not very professional, he thought. But he had been, and that's all that mattered.

He took a seat in the chair next to the bed, cleared his throat, and weighed the options again. If he brought her back safely, she would need more pills and there was a good chance she wouldn't last the weekend. Whatever good he had done would surely be lost to the instant gratification of eternal silence, and there were more ways to obtain it than just curling up at the bottom of a pool. Hell, the gift shop alone held dozens of seemingly innocuous methods to end one's life. Option one really wasn't an option at all.

If he attempted pain therapy and brought her back, she might be on the road to some kind of recovery, but for all practical purposes she probably wouldn't last the week. She might wander around for a bit, her tolerance to the medication ebbed to the point where her dosage could return to "healthy" levels, but it wouldn't last long enough for her to see in the New Year. Option two was a stopgap, nothing more.

If he made her like him and put all of her pain on ice for the foreseeable future, she would find herself locked in a bathroom somewhere down the road just like he had been, trying to destroy everything within reach. But these new wounds would heal – eventually, although it would seem faster than before – and she would go on with her life, such as it was. The pain and anger caused by the attack would always be there, but it would be deadened without robbing her of her senses. Actually, her senses would be heightened, but she would need to manage them. That he could teach her. It would be like having a new member of the family, something that he had been denied, and if he were being honest, that he had denied himself. It was for the best, really. But this way seemed for the best, too.

He rose halfway from his chair, moved to the bed and bent over so she could hear him. "Eliza...are you there?" He was still a bit hoarse. The fact that his tone was a little deeper was, he figured, an asset.

"Mm-hmm." She was in such a state of peace that he almost wanted to keep her under for the night. But he needed time to walk her through things. Twenty-four hours, if he had that much, was not a lot of time to become accustomed to an entirely new way of living – or un-living, as some there in the hotel might say.

"Is Boris there with you?" he asked quietly. "Is he in the tree?"

"Yes...he's still here."

There was a mark on the side of his head that she hadn't paid attention to before. It looked a little like someone laughing, a cartoon maybe, with its mouth opened super wide.

"Good," continued Dmitrije, "Now I want you to watch him, because he's going to dive into the water soon and when he does you're going to become fully conscious and feel wonderfully refreshed. But Eliza, you're also going to feel very different when you wake up, so listen closely."

He swallowed the lump in his throat. This was not the weekend he had planned. It probably wasn't the weekend she had planned, either.

"When you wake up you're going to feel strong, and all the sad memories of what happened to you and Ryan will be stored far away where they can't hurt you anymore. They will always be there for you to visit, but they won't be able to visit you unless you ask them to. Do you understand?"

"Yes."

"Excellent. Eliza, I'm going to continue to ask you to watch Boris. Watch him closely, now. If you feel something while you do, it's perfectly fine. Your arms may begin to feel warm...your legs and your feet, as well. You may even begin to feel hungry. But understand that it is perfectly normal and that nothing can hurt you. Do you understand what I'm saying?"

"Yes...I understand." Her nose twitched as if it the scent of hydrogen sulfide had given it a tweak.

Dmitrije leaned in close, and Eliza took a deep breath. It was not an anxious one, but one that seemed to convey her desire to inhale life and all its wonders again. And she would, to some extent. She would go on to see and do many things, he was sure of it. She may even love again, although it may take years – decades perhaps – and it would be in a different way. But he knew now that it was possible for her to one-day meet another with whom she connected in ways she never thought possible. And when she did, the nothing that Dr. Radan had promised her would feel more like something than any something ever did before.

Eliza was watching the laughing man on the side of Boris' head when something very strange happened. The tiny clump of feathers that had been his eye suddenly elongated and narrowed, as if he had seen something horrible sliding into the pelican's gullet. His mouth, no longer round and joyful began curling into itself like a burning piece of paper. Inside, Boris' eyes, once golden and protective, were now fierce and fixed.

Then her limbs began to move as if by their own accord. Her arms reached into the air, fingers jutting and then curling, just like the laughing man's mouth. Only now, he and her fingers were screaming. Her legs went straight like sticks, locking her knees and pointing her toes. They felt sharp and ready to impale.

The sand was burning her, too. Something was cooking the cookie dough. Could it be the same thing that was painting the sky red? She thought she might be able to grab one of the clouds that had now appeared, and pull it from the red sky like ripping the guts out of a doll – one that was broken, forgotten, and left to rot in the mud.

Something inside Eliza turned around to face her, daring her, shaking her. No, that wasn't right. It was she that was turning and shaking. She had herself by the throat, shouting for her to wake up and fight! It was time to pick up and show them she was alive, and not forgotten at all.

She felt the flesh of the broken Eliza's throat give way to her fingers as they dug in deeper and deeper. Just when she thought she could feel her spine, she heard the cry. It whipped her head around just in time to see Boris drop from the tree and head towards the water.

Eliza shot straight up into a sitting position, took a quick breath and held it. She spun her head towards the window where Dmitrije was sitting, legs crossed, arms joined by an interlocking of fingers that made a bridge from armrest to armrest. The expression on his face could only be described as blankly contemplating. It gave her neither cause for consignment nor concern. He was just there, and she was here on the bed.

She spun her head back forward and exhaled. Then she looked back again. Dmitrije was in the same position and wearing the same expression, but now she saw someone waiting for her – someone she might have known forever.

"How do you feel, Eliza?" he asked clinically, as if the next question was to tell her where she could deliver the check on her way out.

"I guess, I'm—" she paused for a quick review, "—fine. How long was I out?"

"How long do you think?" This part had never gotten old, for him. It was the one magic trick that he got to enjoy.

"A few seconds, maybe? A minute?" She wanted to ask if they had even started, but didn't want to look any sillier than she already probably did.

"Do you remember what time it was when you first laid down and I told you to close your eyes?"

"Hmm...was it...around three, maybe? Four?" She stopped looking at clocks, as a rule. She tried to remember if it was because they made her feel as if time was slipping away or an eternity had sunk in, but the idea brought up no accompanying feeling. It was like reading the ingredients on a cereal box.

Dmitrije gestured to the clock on the bed stand and said, "Why don't you have a look?"

She leaned over and stretched her neck – *stretched her neck!* – in order to read the gold, digital numbers on the tiniest clock radio she had ever seen. They read "6:39" before turning to "6:40" right before her eyes.

"You're kidding! I was out forrrr..." she held the last word as she tried to do the math in her head, something that should have already been happening, "...wait, how long was it?" It was easier to ask. He probably knew and it was pointless to sit there and work it out. Life was too short. How funny, she thought.

"Approximately one hour and fifty minutes," he said, settling it. "You had quite a nap."

"Huh...wow. Cool."

It was time to run a small test.

"So...hungry?" He tried to make it sound like he had only just thought to ask.

Eliza slowly rolled her eyes in their sockets like a stopwatch waiting for the last runner to cross the finish line.

She widened her eyes and said, "Yesss."

He knew just what to do.

Dmitrije took the basket of bread off of the tray, and placed it on the bed stand. There wasn't enough room for it and both his plate and Eliza's plate, not if they wanted to eat comfortably. It was easy enough to reach, with her on the bed and he across from her on the chair, but he was of the professional opinion that it would go untouched.

He had offered to order for both of them and she had happily obliged, which made things that much easier. She hadn't said a word about pain, neither mental nor physical, and the restful state he had put her in before she woke up was still coddling her senses. There was no telling how long it would hold, or when she would start asking questions. He figured staying in the room for a bit longer was the way forward at this point. She would have no interaction with anyone except her doctor, her friend and a kindred spirit – all of them, of course, being the same person. That would allow her to ease into the transformation. Everything else would come in due time.

She had dug into her steak with the kind of fervor he expected, and hadn't said a word in ten minutes. The sixteen-ounce porterhouse cut was already three-quarters of the way finished. To be young, he thought. They needed so little to perk them up. And how young, she was. Younger than she had been only a few hours ago. In the single instance in the universe that he was aware of, time had verily reversed – in a manner of speaking. It was more accurate to say that its forces on a flesh and blood object had been invariably altered. Somewhere, time had a stone in its shoe.

And yes, the blood; it covered the entire bottom of her plate. She gave each, freshly cut portion on the end of her fork a swim before chewing it to bits and swallowing it down.

"Damn, this is good," she said, cutting a new piece. "I can't believe I'm actually eating rare steak. You were right, Dmitrije, the Wyndorf makes a good one." Each piece that went down made her feel stronger, as if she were building up a wall inside her, brick by brick. Why hadn't she eaten in almost two days? As far as she could tell, eating *rocked.*

She cocked her head slightly to one side, but didn't bother looking up from her plate. "So, Dmitrije…what were you doing while I was out?"

Dmitrije wiped his mouth with his napkin as he thought of something to say. Best to keep it simple.

"I talked with you a bit, of course. Did some light reading. Called down to make sure no one was worried about me, which I must say I was chagrined to learn that no one had been. That's the problem with identifying yourself as a doctor, you see...everyone assumes you're fine." The last part was absolutely true, as was the calling down to check on his station. He had given them the excuse that he had been inspired by talking to a few of his fans and needed to rush up to his room and jot down some ideas before they vanished into the ether. He instructed the convention staff to section off his table and announce that whomever returned tomorrow would get a signed copy of his book at half-price. He hadn't made up his mind whether he would follow through with that promise, but it was nice to know that everyone was happy with the information and that he and Eliza would be left alone. She had already assured that her absence would be respected by instating her honor-system auction – about which, he guessed, she hadn't given a second's thought.

"Cool," she said impassively. "Didn't mean to pry."

"Pry?" he chuckled. "You haven't even asked me what I learned?"

She laughed through her nose as she chewed. "Oh, right," she mumbled. "Well give it to me straight, doc. I can take it."

"Before I do, there a few things to consider. First, knowing what I know won't make things any better. In fact, it may introduce new conflicts."

"Like what?"

"Well, for instance, you may develop a low level internal guilt process, whereby you compare your feelings of happiness and confidence against how you've been taught to feel about tragedy."

"I'll feel bad about feeling good." She decided she would tease him later and ask if psychologists got paid by the word like Shakespeare.

"Something like that, yes. More like a dialog just below the conscious. Most people live with some form of it or another. However, rarely are they given the choice to avoid it, which is what I'm offering you."

"Gotcha." She swallowed the last piece, wiped her mouth and put her fork down hard announcing her conquest to the world.

"Just tell me this, then...did I try and stop them?"

He was relieved to hear the Eliza he had known before the procedure coming through her question. There was so much worth keeping and no way of telling how much would be inadvertently packed away in cold storage with the hazardous bits. Sure, the contents of her being had been smothered by an inability to balance reality with expectation – wherein one finds every girl's folly: a little thing called romance – but what had happened to her was not that much different than what had happened to him. He had loved and been helpless in its losing, although his horrors were experienced on a larger, almost numbing scale. Dozens in his care had been slaughtered, including the woman he dare not love but behind closed doors for fear of humiliation. That denial had cost him a piece of his soul. But despite a shame so virulent – so *definite* – he had walked away under his own power. Eliza did not. It made what he was going to say that much more satisfying.

"Yes, Eliza," he said, looking into her eyes. There was a shiny new bit of steel behind them, and they bore into him in search of the truth. "You fought with everything you had."

How he wished he could say the same.

Dmitrije managed to sneak into the bathroom with a change of clothes before Eliza could see the aftermath of his administration. He tried to clean up, but it was useless. The place was a total disaster. Two-and-a-half-feet of the five-foot mirror lay in jagged pieces on the floor and in the tub. The metal towel rack was in the sink, and the curtain rod was bent like a pretzel and evidently shoved several times into the ceiling until it finally caught hold of something and stayed there. He must have had the presence of mind to leave it thinking it might have found a water pipe of some sort. He would claim vandalism, but offer to pay for the damages anyway. *Clap-clap*, Dr. Radan.

It was always peculiar to revisit the scene of one of his tantrums because he barely remembered a thing. There were snapshots and random notions to sift through, but nothing concrete. And there was, of course, the cut on his hand. When she had asked about it he told her he had slipped on some water on the floor. She seemed fascinated by the news. He wondered how she would have reacted to seeing the cut had she had nothing to eat in front of her.

Knowing her, she would have been forthright about any prickles in her esophagus. After all, she was a nicer person than him from the start. Still, he was once again relieved that she had just filed the news away to some remote drawer never to be opened again unless by accident. It was, without a doubt, for the better. He didn't think she was quite ready for a full explanation.

Using the remaining half of the mirror, he weaved a comb through his head one last time, and splashed on a bit of cologne from a bottle on the vanity that had miraculously managed to remain in one piece.

"I'll need to get some fresh clothes too, I think," Eliza said loudly from the other room so he could hear her. "But they're in my car."

"Pity we didn't get them earlier," Dmitrije replied. "Shall I call down and have someone bring them to your room?"

She didn't answer, which made him curious. He emerged from the bathroom, pulling the door closed behind him and found her sitting on the edge of the bed, staring at the floor.

"Sorry…was that a bad idea?"

"No, it's okay. I just haven't been there yet."

"Oh?" He tried to sound only mildly curious, and began collecting his things from the desk.

"Ryan and I always booked the same room. Room 718. It was where we met…sort of. I guess I was avoiding it for as long as I could. Stupid, huh?" She had to admit that it did feel a little silly, now.

"Not at all. Would you like me to go with you?"

She looked up at him with sore eyes. This would be a very big test, he thought. There was no telling what visiting the room would trigger.

"Would you mind?" she asked. "I could get a friend to bring up my stuff."

Dmitrije was worried about inviting a friend, but in a sense it was better than a member of the hotel staff. Especially if she reacted like he did when tripping back in time.

"I don't mind at all," he assured her.

They walked silently down the hall through the gauntlet of revelers. It was Saturday night and everything had kicked into high gear. If Friday night was hymns and handshakes, Saturday night was high mass. There would be bands downstairs in more than one location, and a second ballroom would be hosting the costume contest. Even now, there were Predators crisscrossing rooms, Frankenstein was carrying a bucket of ice, and a pair of white gorillas with giant fangs had entered the elevator and, more considerate than their appearance would suggest, held the door for them.

The trip down to the 7th floor was just as suitably freakish. A coven of gorgeous witches had gotten on at floor 16, only to get off again on the 10th floor where they were replaced by someone in an alien costume that had so many appendages he or she had to be helped into the car. It would require another few minutes to go the last three floors as each pause played out with the same scenario: the car would stop, the doors would open, and a crowd of ghouls would see he, Eliza and the alien standing there with apologetic expressions. Several seconds later it became mutually agreed among all present that it was best to let the car go, and one floor down it would happen again.

They exited the elevator at the 7th floor, and walked at a leisurely pace to the door marked 718. Eliza produced a key from her hoodie pocket and placed it into the slot. The green light came on with a buzz and Eliza removed the card, pulled down on the knob/handle and pushed on the door. Dmitrije held it open with his hand so that she could enter and place the card into the little slot on the wall that would allow her to operate the main lights. Then she hit the switch and the interior space jumped into a warm glow.

Dmitrije stayed outside the room for a few moments as he watched Eliza take a few steps towards the bed. He thought she might want to acclimate to the surroundings with a brief, private ceremony of sorts, and he wanted to respect her ownership of the space.

Eliza arrived at the bed and gave the comforter a feel with her hand.

"It's cool," she said. To the touch, she meant. Not so much the other way.

Dmitrije entered all the way and closed the door behind him, shutting out the sounds of the other guests. Once inside, the silence took over and made room for the past.

Eliza visited the window next and pulled open the curtain. She looked out at the car park below, noticing one person after the other carrying luggage to and from the hotel. Some were alone, some were in groups, and a few, she remarked to herself, were in pairs. How lucky, for them. They appeared to be having a great time.

She pulled the curtain shut and stepped away from the window. She spun around and looked at the desk, taking it in high and low. There was nothing at all remarkable about it and that's exactly why she needed to see it. But before long it began to take on its own significance. It held one of everything: one room service menu, one pen, one "do-not-disturb" sign, one lamp and of course, one chair. Next to it, on a black, metal stand, was a flat screen television. On top of the television, was a single, black remote control.

Eliza felt a tingle down her spine and for the first time since she had awakened from her somnambulistic state, she accepted that she wouldn't be feeling any physical pain. In the back of her mind she had been waiting for the other shoe to drop, but it wasn't dropping. If that was the case, why wasn't she overjoyed?

She grabbed the remote and held it in her hand. It felt light, insubstantial. It was almost pathetic. She looked closely at the buttons and how they had been designed to make the person using it believe they held such awesome power at their fingertips. They could turn the POWER of the TV on and off with a simple touch of a red button. They could START, STOP, REWIND, FAST FORWARD, GO BACK, pull up a MENU, go UP, DOWN – all while they laid on their lazy, fat asses. They probably had games on here, too. Who the fuck comes to a hotel in Florida to play fucking video games, she wondered. What kind of fat, useless kid is so fucking bored in Orlando, of all places, that he makes the decision to play a video game in his hotel room. The fat little fucking bastard should be outside, doing something. It didn't even matter what it was. Anything would be better than festering like an irritating, obnoxious little slug. If she were the little fuck's mother, she would yank the remote from his pudgy little hand, which was probably covered with ketchup and French fry grease and—

Dmitrije watched Eliza reach back with a range of motion most professional athletes would covet and throw the remote across the room. It struck the wall above the bed and exploded into a dozen pieces, which dispersed themselves evenly about the floor just as the laws of physics demanded. Once the energy of the act had completely dissipated, she appeared to relax. But any hope that she was finished was false. With a howl she placed both hands on top of the television and pulled it towards her so that it would fall forward onto the screen. Dmitrije thought to leap into action to keep it from crashing on her foot, but she had jumped back too quickly for that to happen. He wouldn't have made it in time anyway.

Eliza noticed that the screen didn't break – the carpeting was too soft – and that annoyed her. She needed to know that she had hurt it somehow, so she grabbed the cable that was attached to the back of the unit and pulled on it, plucking it from where it was attached like a tiny root from some loose soil. With another yank across her chest the other end of the cable came flying out of the wall. She was temporarily satisfied as she held it in the air. She had ripped out its spinal cord and it was finally dead.

Dmitrije could have guessed her next move. He had done it once himself, and it made for a dramatic disruption in the appearance of the room. She took hold of a clump of comforter in the center of the bed with both hands and yanked it off. With a toss (and another screech), she was rid of it and went again for the sheets underneath. He remembered it feeling like removing the skin of some large animal. The way she looked at the bare mattress made him think that she wanted to humiliate the bed more than flay it, thus destroying it from the inside out rather than vice versa. Once it was naked and vulnerable, she lost interest and stood breathing heavily, shoulders rising and falling. Her hair had taken to covering the entire front of her face as she slowly scanned the room for her next victim.

Knock-knock-knock-knock-knock. Dmitrije turned, placed an eye over the peephole, and saw a young man with tousled black hair looking back at him. It appeared as if he was holding something by its handle in each hand. This must have been the young man she had spoken to before they left his room.

"I believe your things are here, Eliza. What would you like me to do?" He watched as she threw her hair back with a jerk of her head. At least she had heard him.

"Open it." Her voice dripped with equal parts malice and hate.

"Are you sure?" Dmitrije asked, trying not to insult her. "I could go outside and get them for you."

"Why?" She challenged.

"Eliza, look around you. Do you really think he will come and go without asking any questions? At the very least, I'm sure he'll wonder why I'm in here with you."

Dmitrije watched as she thought about it for a few breaths and took a couple of steps towards him. He held his ground. She didn't appear to be interested in attacking him – she could've done that already – but he reminded himself that if he needed to he could overpower her, hopefully without hurting her.

"Let me talk to him," she said.

Dmitrije stepped to one side and Eliza set the chain lock, twisted the handle, and pulled on the door until it was held fast by the four inch length of silver segments. She leaned a single eye into the narrow opening.

"Hey!" Francis said. "I got your stuff."

"Right."

"You gonna open th—"

"Just drop it and I'll get it," she said, looking him over. "I'm naked."

The way she said it, Dmitrije noticed, wrung every ounce of sexuality from the statement.

Francis placed the bags on the ground and looked into the wood of the door.

"Sorry," he said, his enthusiasm crushed. "You coming down? I think I saw a couple of people making bids at your table."

"Later," she said. "Thanks for the stuff."

"If you want me to keep an eye on things, I can. Whatever you want." He used a hand to brush back a forelock of hair, but it just returned to where it was.

"Sure," she said, clenching a fist. "Now I gotta get dressed. Like I said…thanks."

"No problem," said Francis, shrugging. "I'll keep my ringer on high in case you need, like…um…anything." He took a step backward from the door.

Dmitrije had heard him stammer and could only imagine what he was seeing in her single eye that threw him. Had she used them both, she would have ripped out his tongue.

“Okay,” said Eliza, impatiently. “See you later.”

Francis turned and headed for the elevator. Eliza could tell that he wanted to stay and talk some more, but she didn’t think it was because he wanted to see her naked. It was something else. Fuck it, she thought, and closed the door, unset the chain, pulled it open again and took hold of the bags. With a tug of both arms, they were safely inside.

Dmitrije gave her wide berth as she walked to the center of the room, tossed the bags on the bed and sat at its edge.

“What a fucking joke,” she said at last.

“What’s a joke, Eliza?” He wanted to get her talking right way. Oddly, her friend seemed to pull her together somewhat. She had even thanked him twice, which had demonstrated a very rapid return to compassion. Had that been him after his first outburst, he would have had to speak to him through the door if he could have spoken at all.

She didn’t answer.

“What’s a joke?” he repeated.

She began unzipping one of the bags, and yanking out clothes. “Everything. It’s all so stupid. This room, the memories…they’re not real. Even what happened isn’t real. Yeah, it happened, but it wasn’t happening now so why should I give a shit?”

“Do you?” He felt bolder about probing now. Eliza wasn’t an angry person, which is to say she hadn’t been born with that sort of predisposition. She was going to do well if she could get her mind around how things change, some in monumental ways, and that it’s okay to accept that.

“I don’t know, exactly,” she said, pulling a pair of pants from the unzipped bag and placing them on the bed beside her. “Ryan is gone and I got raped. Before that, he and I used to come to this room and have fun. Sure, the no-good fuckers who ruined all of that should die, but I don’t understand why there has to be so much drama surrounding it.”

She stood up and started removing her clothes. The ice was working, Dmitrije thought. Her anger was under control now, she hadn’t ripped out Francis’ throat just because he was there, and it was pretty clear her sense of shame had gone into a deep, deep sleep.

“Perhaps I should step outside and wait for you?” Dmitrije said, politely. "When you're finished we could go and have a drink. What do you say?"

"Or you could just wait, Dr. Hot Pants, and stop looking so shy." Her voice had the nihilistic lilt of a prostitute, but without the thinly veiled lack of self-respect. "I'm sure it's not the first time you've seen a woman's body."

"Of course, not." She was right, but it had been a very long time. It had been even longer since he had seen the lovely, nubile form of a woman as young and beautiful as she.

"Then have a seat, Dmitrije." It could have been an order. "I'll be two minutes."

He crossed the room, took a seat in a thick chair by the head of the bed and began observing her quietly. He was pleased that her pale skin had retained its delicate, olive coating, and he delighted in how he could see the fine bones of her sternum every time she threw back her shoulders. She was undernourished, but her body moved in beautiful synchronization – each motion requiring a fine counter motion that made pulling off a thin t-shirt something done with the hips and legs as well as the arms and the torso. There was no question that she was comfortable in her skin. That may have been the most dramatic change in her yet. Was she enjoying him watching her? It looked as if she might be. If she was, he could consider it a triumph if only she knew the entire truth. He would have to tell her soon, but he wasn't such a fool to not wait until the timing was perfect. There were other obstacles to come, and he would need to see how she handled getting around them.

She disappeared into the bathroom and he could hear her dumping the contents of a small makeup case onto the vanity. Then came the smells, and the sound of running water. It was an orchestra of the female condition, and it broke his heart in its sublime familiarity. He knew at that moment why he had been so compelled to help her. Yes, she was lovely and her anguish had awakened in him a very primal instinct, but there was more to it than that. She was proof that much of the old Dmitrije Radan still remained inside. He always knew he was there, but over the years the memory of him had become little more than a faint hint of smoke rising from damp, smoldering cinder. He wanted to share the news of this remnant of humanity with her, as he thought it would help. Again, it would have to wait.

The sound of a long zipper (and then another) perked him up in his chair. Seconds later, Eliza appeared from inside the bathroom and stopped to adjust herself. Apparently something had shifted off center – from sitting, he guessed. She had fixed her hair long and straight like night rain, and how it shined. She wore a clinging dress that started tight around her neck then cut in to expose a jealous portion of shoulder before it dripped along her hips and seamlessly forged into a pair of fishnet leggings. Then there were the fingerless gloves that extended up into her middle arm, made of velvet and with a narrow touch of lace trim. Dmitrije eventually worked his way down this stunning nocturnal celebration to where he saw the source of the zippers: black boots, shiny and sharp, with at least four-inch heels. When she had finished aligning whatever it was that had dared relocate, she lifted her head and looked at him. Thick eyelashes, her own with some help, blew an evil kiss over her dark eyes. Below them, beyond the smooth contours of her cheekbones, parted the red lips of his dreams. And like that she stood there, offering him the sovereignty of the moment, but he could do nothing with it. So, unsurprisingly, she took it back.

"Ready, darling," she said, channeling more actress than lover.

"Indeed," Dmitrije replied as he stood up from the chair. Despite his knees going a little weak, he felt as if he were wearing a suit of armor.

Saturday

part five

Dmitrije watched as the numbers representing hotel floors subtracted by one. So many authors had used the trip down in an elevator as a metaphor for one's descent into madness. It was a hackneyed and amateurish attempt at storytelling in his opinion, and he was pleased to have avoided it successfully. He preferred to let something small and seemingly innocuous give the clue to the reader that the hero was doomed. However, at that moment, he couldn't help thinking that his own descent meant precisely the opposite. Traveling down embodied a form of virtue in this case, as if an unblemished part of him were being laid back into a soft, velvet case where it would be protected, yet still accessible. He chanced a look out of the corner of his eye to where Eliza was standing. She looked incredibly beautiful. It was the kind of beauty that caused an admirer terrific pain. She would hurt many souls in the future, he hoped. It was her turn.

There was a *ding* and the elevator doors pulled apart. Several people were waiting patiently to get on and all backed away, forming what reminded him of a bridal path. What he wanted was to be with her, but not as her husband. That could never work. At the moment he was happy and proud to be her mentor and confidant. That could take him to the end of his days.

She strode into the very center of the lobby, stopped and said, "So…what the hell are we drinking?"

Dmitrije was still catching up to her when he answered. "I

think I could stand a brandy," he said, pointing to the restaurant bar. "There looks as good a place as any."

She snuck her arm under his, locking it firmly. "Let's do it."

They entered the bar and a dozen conversations were interrupted. Half of those, Dmitrije wagered, would be lost. How extraordinary it was.

"You want to go to the bar or find a table?" asked Eliza. Before he could answer she blurted, "I know! There!" She pointed to a small couch in the rear of the room. It was the same couch he had chosen last evening.

"Perfect," he chimed. "My favorite spot."

They cut across the floor and took their places on the soft cushions. Eliza waved one leg over the other with a languid hike of her right boot, and crossed her arms. Dmitrije watched as she surveyed the area. Again, he tried to assess what she could be thinking. The place was slowly filling up, but it was still easy to see everyone who had arrived. Not one escaped her judgment.

"Decided what you're having, my dear?" he asked.

"Not exactly...I've always been a light beer girl but suddenly I'm liking what *she's* drinking." She pointed a long finger at a pixie-cute blonde who was giggling at a young man that had to be her boyfriend. The two were close and her large eyes were twinkling like novas. In her hand she held a highball glass filled with some kind of red mixer. A red straw jutted out of the top and spent much of the time approximately one inch from her mouth.

"I suppose we could ask the waiter when he comes to take our order," Dmitrije said. "I'll see if I can get his attention."

"No. I'll do it." Eliza stood up and placed her hands on her hips, looking down at the small table in front of them. Then she raised her boot – the same one she had used to cross her legs – and stepped over it. Without so much as a hop she was on the other side and heading directly for the pixie girl.

Dmitrije felt his first wave of disquiet since she had received her bags. The respite was over. He needed to get back on duty and watch her carefully.

Eliza made good time. She wanted to know what was in that fucking drink. The closer she got, the more delicious it looked.

And when the girl stirred it, she could barely maintain her composure.

"What is that?" Eliza asked, assertively. Her smile should be enough of a hello.

The girl looked down at her drink as if something had fallen into it.

"Umm...I think it's called a red lotus," she said, unsure. She held it closer to Eliza's face. "You want to try it?"

Eliza took the straw into her fingers and placed her lips on the end. She sucked an inch from the glass and let the liquid flush the inside of her mouth before swallowing.

"Ugh...sweet," she said. "You actually *like* that?"

The girl laughed a little and said, "It's okay. If you're looking for something less sweet, maybe you should try a vodka and club soda."

Her boyfriend said, "Or whiskey. Manhattans taste like shit, but they'll get you bombed."

Pixie slapped his hand. "Don't try and get her drunk."

"No, I don't want to get drunk," Eliza said. "I just want something...*red*."

The girl laughed again and said, "Okay...um...what about a Bloody Mary? Ever have one of those?"

Eliza's eyes widened and she placed a hand near her throat. "Where do I get one?"

"The bar?" asked Pixie, skeptically. "Just walk over to that guy...he's called *the bartender*...and I'm sure he'll be happy to make one for you. Tell him not to make it too spicy, though."

"Okay," Eliza said, wheeling around. The drink sounded wonderful. She'd heard of it, of course, but for some reason forgot all about it – probably because she never had one. But then why couldn't she think of a single other drink name? She turned back around to the girl and said, "Thanks. I'll let you know how it is."

"You do that," the boyfriend said.

Pixie slapped him again and they both laughed.

Across the room, Dmiitrje told the waiter what he wanted and asked that it be put on his room charge. Once the extremely busy-looking man was gone, he had a look over at the table where the girl and her boyfriend were collecting their things. Eliza was gone.

He stood up and looked around. A large group of ghouls had just come in and they all ran straight to the multicolored taps that poked up proudly like flags at a parade. Kids having fun consistently trumped old man on the brink, and he scolded himself for letting her out of his sight. He left the couch and headed for the bar.

He saw her speaking to the bartender, and it looked as if the handsome young man in the black vest couldn't understand what she was saying. Dmitrije wondered if perhaps he was too ready to see things that weren't there. It was possible. What was also possible was that Eliza was growing confused, and that wasn't a good thing. He made his way through the excited crowd and eventually fell in behind her.

"Everything alright?" He directed his question at the bartender who was looking cross.

"Ask her," he said, referring to Eliza. "Everything I give her she hates."

"He's not listening," she said. "And he can go fuck himself if he thinks I'm going to drink this dishwater." She was talking about the three glasses in front of her. The contents of each were virtually identical, save one or two small details: one looked slightly darker, one had a stick of celery, and the one in her hand had no ice.

"I'm sure we can work something out," Dmitrije said. He put his hand on Eliza's shoulder. "Why don't you come with me?"

"I'm not going anywhere! She was staring directly at the bartender, who was beginning to lose patience. "I want...my fucking...drink."

"I'll get you a drink, Eliza. Please." He could feel her skin become warm under his hand, as if her blood were attacking it. "And put those on my room charge," he said to the bartender. "Room 1803."

Eliza got mad. "Don't kiss his ass!" she said.

"I'm trying to get you what you want," he told her. "And this is not the way."

She stopped and stared into his eyes. He couldn't afford to budge or waver at all. If he did, there's no telling how far this would escalate.

"I can get you what you want if you let me," he said to her, without a shred of levity.

Eliza looked back to the bartender. "Fuck off," she frothed.

The bartender held his tongue and began taking away the glasses.

Dmitrije shot him a sympathetic smile and lead Eliza out through a council of satanic bishops.

Once outside, Eliza turned to him. "What the fuck is wrong with you?"

"Nothing is wrong with me, Eliza. But we do need to talk." He held her arms just below the shoulders, gently but with a certain amount of authority.

Eliza let off a little explosion. "Talk? I thought we came down here to drink? We talked all fucking day!"

"Yes, but that will have to wait. Please. You must trust me."

Eliza could finally see he wasn't just trying to avoid an embarrassing scene. Something was definitely up. And if she were going to get her goddamn "drink on" in this century, she had better play nice and do what he says.

Dmitrije never thought they'd make it. Even when he let them into his room and closed the door behind them, doubts followed him like persistent wraiths through gaps in the air vents. The elevator ride was exhausting. People kept coming off and on and all Eliza wanted to do was cause them some manner of harm. And then there were the looks from boys. She had told more than one to do things that he, as an author, couldn't have dreamt up. On one occasion she told a pair of ogling ogres to get plague of the eyes and fuck themselves with fire. Is that even possible? He had to apologize to no fewer than twenty people, and then for each one of them he had to apologize to Eliza. She was beginning to spiral out of control, and despite knowing it was coming, he could never have predicted that she would react quite this way.

And now she was pacing in front of the window, throwing him looks that nearly set the curtains aflame.

"What the fuck is going on, Dmitrije?" she yelled.

"Eliza, please try and calm down. I can explain."

"No...I'm through calming down!" She had taken to combing her hair back with her fingers, sending it wildly into the air. "And I'm sick of the doctor bullshit. I swear...if you try any more Scanners mindfuck shit with me I will fucking trash this place."

He removed his jacket and threw it down on the bed. It was time to ratchet things up a notch. “And if you don’t calm down and do as I say you will never learn what you want to know. Where will that leave you, eh? Who else will you attack?”

She froze at the word attack.

“There are things to discuss,” he continued, “and we can’t do that if I have to constantly deal with this behavior. We will never get anywhere.”

Eliza combed through her hair one last time and fell back into the chair by the window – the very chair from which he had brought Eliza the Terrible into the world.

“Thank you,” he said, taking a seat on the bed. “Now…there is a combination of things happening at once inside you, so let me start at the beginning so that you understand.” He was starting to sweat, and undid the cuffs of his shirt. “I believe the rage you are feeling is leftover from your memory recovery. It doesn’t always come out in a single purge. Sometimes it requires several episodes, and unfortunately they can happen at any time. I was doing my best to help you manage it but…perhaps I overlooked a few things.”

She crossed her arms. “What things?”

It could have been worse. At least she was asking questions.

“Eliza, I’m going to show you something. But I want you to promise me you will do exactly as I say. It must be this way or I’m afraid we won’t be able to continue.” He loosened his collar, and prepared himself for her answer. “Well…will you do it?”

“Yes,” she grunted. “I can’t stand this waiting!”

Dmitrije left the bed and opened the small refrigerator. With a deep breath, he withdrew the leather pouch and closed it again. Once back on the bed, he unzipped it and reached in. He knew there were four vials left, and he had purposely skipped his five o’clock to conserve. He picked one without looking, took it out, and placed the pouch on the bed.

Eliza twisted her face in disgust. “What the hell is that?”

Dmitrije held it out to her.

After a few seconds, she leaned forward and snatched it from his hand.

He watched as she looked it over. There were only so many ways to hold it, only so many angles to try.

She looked at him, and he could see her eyes beginning to grow moist. She said, “Is this...blood?”

Dmitrije nodded his head.

Eliza rose from the chair and walked closer to the light. She held the vial in her palm and rolled it carefully around. What the fuck is going on, she wondered. Why couldn’t she say anything? Why wasn’t she throwing this disgusting shit back in his face? Why did she—

“Go on, Eliza...open it.” He stared at the carpet, a bad boy who had been caught sneaking his father’s wine.

Eliza saw the first tears hit her hand near where the vial was resting. It wasn’t until after they started to fall steadily that images and random bits of information began rushing into her head. She was unable to make sense of any of it. It was like trying to breathe with one’s head out the window of a car going hundreds of miles per hour. There was only one person who could sort it all out for her, but he was the last person she wanted to hear speak.

Dmitrije wiped the sweat from his brow and said, “I can help.”

“Shut the fuck up!” she screamed.

She ran to the mirror and opened her mouth, looking around inside. Everything in there looked the same. She closed it and said, “What the fuck is this, some kind of joke? What the fuck did you do to me?”

Eliza twisted around to see as much of her neck as possible. It, too, was perfectly preserved. Then she held the vial up and gnashed at it, letting go a ferocious cry.

“I can explain if you—“

She cut him off with a loud slap to the face that he didn’t see coming.

“What did you do to me? Tell me, you fucking bastard!” She screamed at him, covering him in a choleric shower of spit.

With a swift upward motion of his hand he squeezed her mouth closed, pinching in both cheeks. Here eyes popped open, red with rage and with what she was. She was still holding the vial when he lifted her a few inches off the ground, forcing her to grab one of his wrists with her free hand as she rose up on the pointy toes of her boots. She appeared to be in a significant degree of discomfort, but would not drop the vial.

Dmitrije held her there, his eyes peering into her soul and destroying every bit of evidence that Dr. Radan had ever existed.

"That will be enough, Eliza. No more. You will listen now, and you will do so while remaining quiet and calm. You will do this because there are things that I must tell you that you will need to know to survive...things that I could never explain to the girl I met in the theater. That girl is gone. Dead. As dead as autumn leaves. She died on the shore of an estuary with the man that she loved and that is all there is to it. I tried to help her...*wanted* to help her...but I finally had to let her go. I've replaced her with the girl I see before me and the one you are now. If you wish, she can die, too. But not without first hearing who she is...what she is...and what exactly she can do. And she will hear these things without screaming, hitting, or acting out in any way. Do I make myself perfectly clear? And I mean *perfectly* clear."

He watched her eyes relax in a sign of capitulation. It wasn't how he wanted to do things. He never had any desire to overpower her. But then again, he had no experience in such matters. He had never taken someone's humanity away from them, with or without their permission. He had only seen it done, over and over again, without the slightest intention of giving something back.

Eliza sat very still as she heard all about her new *un*-life. Her conscious mind didn't believe that she would need to drink blood – *monsters aren't real, they're on eBay* – and yet she held onto the vial so tightly there had been several times where she thought she might crush it into wet dust. She knew she wasn't feeling any pain and that she felt physically strong. When Dmitrije had reminded her of how she had yanked the TV cable from the wall, she remembered how easy it had been to do it. There was something fundamentally different about how she felt inside, too. She could only describe it as a combination of indifferent peace and rabid anger. Playing back the events of the last few hours created an image in her head of, of all things, a slinky. Her father had given her one as a kid, and she used to love making it climb down the stairway into the basement. What usually happened was that it stopped after a few steps because it hadn't cleared the next ledge and all the rings collected into a single stack. But with some practice you could find just the right spot so that it cleared each step and the rings shifted smoothly from one end to the other until it made it all of the way to the floor. And in a way that's what he was telling her that she needed to do: practice finding the right spots. It was possible, he said, to add just the right amount of passion to her resting state in order to approximate love, desire, and even joy. He nearly wept when he said she had taught him a tenderness that challenged everything he ever believed about himself. It was also possible to address the more polemic pole so that it, too, would acquire different shades – everything from the murderous rage that she was familiar with, to a mild distaste that she could conceal. Time, he said, would be kind. On the one hand, she would need lots of it; on the other, she would have plenty if she were careful.

There was still the matter of how she had been turned. She hadn't found any marks. There were still places she could look, but she knew her body – more intimately now, it seemed – and she was absolutely positive there would be nothing to find when she did. Still, it would have been much easier to believe his words if there had been a scar, or a hint of sharpness to any one of her thirty-two teeth. All she had was a raw trust in him and a vial in her hand that she had no intention of letting go.

She could see that he wanted to go on as there were, he said, more "practical" issues to address, but her head was spinning and her bout of seething had given her disorienting tunnel vision.

"Dr. Radan...can we stop for a little?" she asked, pulling the fist with the vial close to her chest. "I need to take a walk or something to, I don't know...let some of this sink in." She immediately regretted the expression. It was all getting very surreal.

He leaned back, as if to give her more personal space. "So I'm Dr. Radan, now, am I?"

"Sorry," she mumbled. Then she stood up, her arms still folded. "You saved my life – sort of – so I guess I can't be too mad at you. I just don't know how to look at you now. I don't even know how to look at myself."

"I understand. Eliza, listen...if you can promise me you won't get into any trouble, I don't see why a walk wouldn't be a very good idea. I must warn you, however," he said, looking away shyly, "the chances of you being left alone, dressed the way you are, are rather slim."

"I'll ignore them," she said.

"What if that becomes difficult?"

"I'll come back."

He held her gaze and waited.

"I promise," she said, letting go a small smile. Deception wasn't originally what she had in mind, but it had been so easy she couldn't help herself.

"I suppose it'll be safe," he said, standing. "And only right, really. I'm not your father, Eliza, I'm your friend. I do feel a large responsibility for you, and there are still many important things to share. But even though it was out of...I don't know if *love* is the right word but I guess it will do...I've taken an enormous liberty with your soul. If there is to be a backlash, I'd rather be there when it happens and take my lumps. Does that make sense?"

Something fluttered in Eliza's heart. It was slight, like a tiny moth had escaped. How unusual, she thought, to have an older man want to look after her. She decided that on her walk she would figure out if it was a good feeling or something else. Maybe doing so would begin the process of adding variation to her moods like he had talked about. Then again, she had no idea how she was going to feel about all of this once she walked outside the door and she needed to know right away.

"Yeah...it makes sense," she said, "I just need a little time, if that's cool." She stared down at her boots and noticed how her feet didn't hurt.

"Yes...it's cool," he replied, making the last word sound self-consciously hip.

Eliza threw him another quick smile, and strutted to the door.

"One more thing, if I may," he said, failing to not sound like a high school principal. "That thing you have in your hand is very powerful. If you're thinking of using it, do an old man a favor and think again, would you?"

Eliza had become so attached to the vial she had forgotten it was still in her clutches. She accepted how it must have looked.

"Here," she said, tossing it towards him, "you hold onto it."

Dmitrije caught it with only a slight bobble.

"Think of it as insurance," she added. Then she opened the door and left.

Eliza was happy to be rid of the vial – well, the feeling was *like* happy. Everything she was feeling was more *like* the feeling she remembered than the actual feeling; everything except rage, of course. But the vial had been controlling her, and she needed to be free of it if she was going to figure out what the hell was really happening. She thought of a parasite, but it conjured images of blood sucking and brought her back to square one. Her intention was to try and act as normally as possible, and to do that she felt she needed to put everything that was in room 1803 behind, including Dr. Radan.

She walked along the hall, listening to the muffled sounds of merriment behind each door as she passed. If what he was saying was true, that would no longer be her, she thought to herself. Only, hadn't she already left that behind? To be in a room full of friends and laughing at stupid stuff was a fond memory, but its potential as an event in her life had been snuffed out long before she made the trip to Orlando. She came here for money and nothing more. It had been a huge challenge and an even bigger risk and she had failed and succumbed respectively. How strange it was, she thought, being able to review one's death and doing it looking so fierce. She wasn't yet comfortable with the concept, but it was getting easier to roll it around in her head. Maybe if she faced the reality of her death completely, what she was – what Dr. Radan was trying to get her to believe they *both* were – would finally take root. If she wasn't happy with what she saw, she supposed she could always make the decision to die again, couldn't she? She thought he had said as much. Could she drive a stake through her heart? He hadn't said anything like that. Was dying even an option? Hell, could she fly?

She laughed at the absurdity of the thought, shook her head and it was gone. She would see for herself if she were able to believe, accept and even embrace all that she had learned. And damn it, she was walking in her favorite heels without a limp so it couldn't be all bad. In fact, she would take the stairs.

Eliza pushed on the bar of the stairwell door and it opened with a *ker-chunk* that echoed off the colorless tiles. She had no idea where it would leave her at the bottom, but she assumed she would figure out where she needed to go once she got her bearings.

As she descended, there was a palpable, incremental shift in her attitude. The click and clack of her heels seemed to suggest the steady movement of an internal timer, marking some sort of transformation. She was aware of all that she still didn't know, but it was impossible not to notice a few minor things here and there that were, for lack of a better word, awesome. According to the big "7" on the door – it occurred to her why she noticed it but it didn't matter – she had just gone down eleven flights of stairs without feeling the least bit tired or breaking into a single bead of sweat. The remaining floors went by in much the same way. There was one moment when she had caught an old man sneaking up a flight of stairs in his boxers, and he nearly tripped. She wondered at the time if she would have helped him. By the next half a flight she decided she probably would have giggled a "sorry" and kept going.

She reached the bottom and opened the door. The carpet down here was blotchy and in pretty bad shape. As long as her heels didn't catch, she didn't care. Once she got to where she was going, it made sense.

The glass doors slid open and she took her time walking through them. Once again, the area was empty. Apparently the sign that was now staring at her with those plastic letter things that were stuck onto one of those felt board things was telling her that she must turn around immediately and that the cameras would catch her if she didn't. Bullshit, she thought. Like they were paying someone to watch those cameras, if they even worked.

She traversed the patio, stood at the edge of the pool and looked into it. It was filled with water. The water was still. There was a light on in the deep end that was turning the whole thing radioactive green. Some debris had collected at the bottom drain: leaves, from what she could tell, and your basic pieces of dirt. She could hear the fountain as she had before. She remembered it had calmed her a bit before she took that big step.

She tried to put her head back into that space, not because she wanted to feel her despair again but just to see if she could. But she could no more feel the Eliza that had wanted to die any more than she could feel the one before her that had loved life so much. They were two different people, neither of which had anything to do with her now. No, that wasn't right. There were still memories. Some of them winked at her from a remote place in her mind, as if they wanted her to know that everything was okay. It could have been her new attitude that was making her think the old Elizas approved of what she was, but until she was able to talk to them, false justification would have to do.

An unpleasant indignation flooded behind her eyes where perhaps a blessed misery would have done so before. It was, she concluded, the calling card of her new survival instincts. No one ever told her, not that she could remember, that one had to be loving all the time or gentle and kind. Okay, maybe she had heard it from this authority figure or that talk show host but who was to say they weren't just bullshitting her so that life would be easier for them? Maybe life really was about telling little lies here and there and to oneself in order to stay on the path – which, ironically, meant she had been onto the truth from the start. She never minded the nickname, neither of them. Lies and Love All: it was a formula for survival. It had been all along. And now she had found a new one – or it had found her, both perhaps – and she had needed to kill the old Eliza to be able to use it.

Death so that one could live; she liked that.

Dmitrije stood at his window, looking down at the pool below. The roof was closed, just as it had been before, but he could see enough through its brown, tinted glass to know what was going on and that it was okay.

He reached up into his mouth. The sensation was slight but constant.

Eliza heard the doors open, followed by a woman's nervous laughter. She didn't turn around, but continued to listen as the familiar voice of a man taunted the woman with promises of sincerity delivered in a horrid form of baby talk. It was the kind of baby talk that some men used to soften the true nature of their intentions. In fact, the word "baby" is used a lot. He was using it now. It objectified her, as it sought to convince her that she was dear to him while underneath it wanted her to feel weak and helpless. It was, in reality, like the poison that venomous creatures used to paralyze their prey. How clear that was to her now.

She turned to see Dane Harding checking her out. He had Lorena by the hand and was pulling her towards him but he wasn't looking at her. He was looking at Eliza – the new Eliza.

"Whoah!" said Dane, letting Lorena slip from his fingers, nearly causing her to fall. He never looked back to check. "What are *you* doing out here by yourself?"

Eliza watched as Lorena rubbed her upper arm and stifled a moan.

"Thinking," she said. And she was. She was looking at Lorena, who was looking back at her imploringly, and trying to put it all together. She was also fully aware that Dane was heading towards her, and that he was clearly drunk.

"Thinking?" he asked, but not really. "Well you know what *I'm* thinking? I'm thinking you should join our little party, that's what *I'm* thinking." He continued to walk towards her, puffing out his chest and pulling his pants up by the belt. He had an oversized buckle with a "skull and crossbones" made of rhinestones on the front. Yep, it was right there, reflecting the radiation, just a few inches above where his cock was supposed to be.

Eliza turned to Lorena, who she thought might be in danger. She wasn't sure. She was listening to a sharp intuition that felt as though it was beaming out from her tongue, of all places. Yes, that was it. She could taste the bitter tang of pain, and it was coming straight from where Lorena was standing.

"What kind of party?" asked Eliza.

"Our kind of party, sweetheart. Lorena wants to party, too, but she's having a little trouble understanding that."

"Fuck off," Lorena barked. "I'm not a fucking whore."

"You mean you were going to *charge* me?" he said, laughing. "You should fucking *pay* me."

"Don't listen to him," Lorena said to Eliza, "he's drunk...and a fucking jerk."

"Oh, now I'm a fucking jerk?" He took a few threatening steps towards Lorena. "Who was the one who wanted to 'take a walk', huh? Who was the one who was flashing her fucking tits at me all day?"

Lorena looked shocked. "Flashing my tits at you? Maybe you were looking down my shirt when I bent over," she said defiantly, "but just because you're trying to convince yourself you like women don't go and blame me."

Eliza nearly chuckled. So Lorena saw it, too. Not that it was a big deal if true, but he clearly wasn't beyond making people uncomfortable in his effort to deny it. She nearly said something to that effect when Dane growled and charged the ex-soap star. It reminded her of those "most shocking videos" programs on television where someone with a camcorder tapes something horrific and gasps like a sissy through the whole thing instead of lifting a finger to help. That always made her sick. Everything was a fucking show, anymore.

She barely thought the words "show's over" when she felt her legs moving, heading in Dane's direction. She was too late to stop him from shoving Lorena into a few chairs and sending her to the ground. Could she stop him from doing anything else? She asked herself that question as she watched Dane pull Lorena up by her shirt, exposing a pretty, black bra. The funny part was that the question hadn't come from her but from one of the little Elizas inside while she was busy checking out Lorena's underwear. Eliza in the awesome, high-heeled boots never felt any doubt, nor did she bother to answer. She just drove one of her stiletto heels into the big queen's ribcage, breaking what must have been a rib. As she watched him collapse into a nearby table, she promised herself that she would never break anything again unless she knew what it was.

Dane howled, and held one of his big hands over the wound. It looked pretty nasty, Eliza thought. There was a good chance he was going to get really angry in about two seconds but that was enough time to help Lorena to her feet and say, "Love your bra."

Dane attacked, hands forward, teeth bared. Eliza dexterously stepped aside and he shot straight past her, almost falling into the pool. He was even drunker then she thought. How funny would it be if a little girl like her survived the deep end but a hulking horse's ass like Dane bumbled into the shallow end and died. That was funny, wasn't it?

Eliza stepped in front of Lorena and steadied herself for another attack. Then she saw something that made her tongue itch: blood – lots of it. She had cut him pretty good and his exertion had fed the wound. Maybe she could talk him into letting her have a little. If he agreed, she might be willing to forget all about tonight.

"You fucking...*cunt*," growled Dane. He looked to take a step, but dropped to one knee instead. He looked down at his shirt where it was dark and shiny. A few seconds later, he was doubled up and lying on his side.

"Oh my God," gasped Lorena.

"I'll go look," said Eliza.

She walked over to Dane and knelt down next to him. He was having trouble breathing, and his eyes were rolling around in his head like he was tracking angels. Ignoring his descent into shock, Eliza reached down and touched the soaked stain.

"Is he alright?" asked Lorena.

Eliza didn't know, nor care. He was nothing at that point but an object that held for her an increasing fascination. She brought two of her fingers up to her face and gazed at the blood that was covering them. Dane was looking in her direction now, but it was unclear if he could see or comprehend what was going on. If he could, he would have been privy to a most unusual sight.

Eliza closed her eyes and put both fingers into her mouth.

The effect was instant. She jumped to a standing position and opened her mouth wide. The scream that she let out put Lorena in a chair.

Inside her head it was all there: the estuary, Boris, the boat, the three men – Ryan. The violence replayed in her head at a blistering pace: STOP, REWIND, PLAY, STOP, REWIND, PLAY. She couldn't turn it off. The brutality was relentless and endless.

Lorena shivered and said, "Honey...m-maybe we should call someone."

Eliza heard only the sound of her cries on that day, and saw only what Boris showed her to do. She dove down onto Dane's limp frame and jammed both fingers deep into his wound.

Dane shot up from the ground like she had accidentally pressed his reset button and put Eliza flat on her back.

Out of his mind, he grabbed Eliza's throat, smearing it with his own blood. But nothing he could do, no amount of pressure he could apply, would stop her from hissing hate into his face and jabbing at his wound. She was driving her fingers in as far as they would go, and she wasn't ever going to quit.

That was when Lorena screamed, covering up the sound of the sliding doors.

Dane reared back a fist, preparing to unleash a devastating strike and promptly fell asleep. His fist, still clenched in fury, froze in the October sky like an ugly meat moon. The man who had most recently portrayed Corporal Punishment in the *Landmine* series had slumped into such a massive heap that it wasn't until Dr. Radan stepped around him that Eliza realized he was there.

"I thought we had an agreement?" he said, lowering Dane's arm and placing it against his wound.

Eliza, her face and neck stained dark red, ripped an impish smile from ear to ear.

Eliza finally had to admit she was tired. It was very late and once she had been able to get rid of Lorena who was very sweet but also very chatty, all she wanted to do was take off her boots and lay down. As it turned out, the soap star was almost legally blind and saw what happened at the pool in very little detail. She knew only the basics: Eliza had come to her rescue, and for that she was eternally grateful. Eliza knew that they were actually "even" now, but didn't bother correcting her.

As she lay in her bed she couldn't help but think about what Dmitrije would say when they met up for breakfast. After he had made it look like Dane hurt himself falling into the tables (instructing him to wake up a few minutes after they left with that very scenario implanted in his memory was fucking impressive) he mentioned to her that there were some things still left to discuss. She wanted to call him again and ask, but the last time they talked he was clearly getting annoyed. Old men need more rest, he said. It made her laugh. She thought he had, as well.

The questions kept dancing around in her head. What else did she need to learn? Would he teach her how to put someone to sleep by just touching them? That would probably have to wait. It looked like it required a lot of practice, and her syllabus – a word he used and had to explain – was already a few pages too long. He did say it was something she may need to learn how to do when she was short on fluids. *Fluids* – it sounded like he was talking about Gatorade or something. The more she thought about it, the less there seemed to be much of a difference between what he meant and what everyone else bought in the store.

Eliza's eyes popped open. She didn't remember what she was thinking about when she fell asleep, but it hadn't disturbed her any. The curtains were drawn tight like Dmitrije had instructed, so she had no idea what time it was. She reached over and turned the clock radio in her direction. It read 11:42. Shit, she was late and *very* thirsty.

She sprung from the bed and tore through her bag looking for her sweats. She found them, still rolled, and laid them out on the bed. Before she zipped the bag back up she caught a glimpse of a few tampons. She wondered if – fuck it, she would find out sooner or later. In thirty seconds she was dressed.

She jerked open the door and ran as fast as her flip-flops would carry her. Some people had already started checking out, and she watched as they tried to squeeze their umpteen suitcases into the elevator. She gathered her hair into a red, fabric tie and pushed into the stairwell.

The steps went by in a blur, and the exit she used put her right outside the central lobby. In a flash she was past the main elevators, through the last-day desperation shoppers, and into the restaurant. She glided past the bar and headed towards the other side where there were tables and booths. He hadn't answered either of his phones so if he wasn't in one of them, she would have to head into the Dealers' Room in her sweatpants. It wouldn't be a big deal, but she didn't feel like doing it.

She turned a corner and looked around. There was a booth in the back that had been set, but looked empty. When she got close she realized that it had been occupied all along, but she couldn't see that someone was there due to the tall back of the bench. She only needed to see his hands to know it was Dmitrije. He was reading the paper, and it looked like he was on a second glass of juice.

Eliza slid in across from him and said, "I'm *sooo* sorry. I was exhausted."

"That's why I told you to set your alarm. You'll never wake up on time when you're under that deep."

He slid a pink juice drink over to her.

"What's that?"

"Pink, I believe."

"I can see that. What's it made of?"

"Grapefruit. And I suggest you drink some of it," Dmitrije advised. "Sleeping is good, but it's not enough." He pointed to the juice and said, "That is *just* enough."

She took a sip and made a face. "Ugh...it's awful."

"I had to pick something," he complained jokingly. "You were late."

"I said I was sorry," she joked back. "So...go ahead. Tell me what I need to know."

The waiter brought over two plates of pancakes and placed them on the table.

Dmitrije put the paper to the side, and picked up his knife and fork.

"Not until we've had breakfast," he said, grinning. "Some things never change."

The waitress refilled Dmitrije's coffee and Eliza assured her that she didn't want any. When she left, Dmitrije took a sip from his cup, reached into his front shirt pocket, and pulled out a business card. Under his name it read "HYPNOTHERAPIST". In one corner there were the customary series of numbers and email address.

"I should probably give this to you now before I forget. It's an old one, but the information is correct. I've written my cell phone number on the back."

Eliza looked on both sides and said, "Right...cool," and tucked it up the right sleeve of her sweatshirt. When she had pulled it on this morning she discovered that she still appreciated the black heart with wings design that was on the front.

"I've a few other things for you, as well...something to hold you over, so to speak, with instructions based on your weight and body mass. It should do until the first parcel arrives at your home address...which I will also need." He pulled out a pen from inside the paper and handed it to her with a small napkin. "Print legibly, please."

"I will, I will," she assured him.

"The other things I've had put safely in your car, along with your belongings from the dealers room. I hope that was alright."

"Yeah, sure," Eliza said. "I didn't want to go back in there and do it, anyway."

He watched her finish writing her address and took the napkin away from her. He read it to make sure he could make out all the letters and numbers, folded it, and placed it neatly into his front pocket. "Thank you."

"So how'd I do?" she asked, holding out her hand.

Dmitrije acted reminded, reached into his front pants pocket, and pulled out a small money clip. He tugged out a wad of bills and laid them on the table in front of her.

Eliza spread the bills out so she could count them.

"Dmitrije...there's a thousand dollars here," she said, arching her eyebrows.

"I'm sorry. Were you expecting dinar?" he replied.

"Knock it off. There's no way I made that much." She counted the bills again.

"Why not?" he asked, feigning insult.

"Because. I didn't even go back to close the bidding. What did they buy?"

"I don't know, I didn't see," he said, placing the clip back into his pants pocket. "I suppose you'll have to work that out when you get home."

"You didn't see? Then how did you get all that shit to the car?" He was driving her mad, but in a fun way.

"I didn't," Dmitrije said. "I had your friend do it. I found him at the pool participating in the traditional 'end of the weekend dip'. I thought I might have dropped my pen out there last night, and as it turns out, I did." He held it up to show her, and slid it into his shirt pocket. "He was very willing, I must say."

"You mean Rufus?" she blurted.

"I thought his name was Francis?" Dmitrije replied. "At least that's what he said."

"It is, I just call him Rufus 'cause...never mind." She would save that one for later.

"Should I not have asked him?" said Dmitrije, rolling up his napkin and dropping it on his plate.

"No, it's cool. He just lives not too far from me in Sarasota, so I hope he doesn't ask to follow me back or anything. He's been a little too helpful and I don't want him to think he needs to take care of me or anything."

The waitress brought over the bill and thanked them.

"So are you staying for the closing ceremonies?" he asked. "I hear they're going to be even more pointless than last year."

"I don't think so. I'm kind of anxious to get home." She fingered the card in her sleeve, but hadn't yet touched the money. "Where are you off to?"

"Me? I fly back to New York for a few days and then I'm off to Vancouver. My agent seems to think I should do a talk show up there. Not sure what good it could do anyone listening to me talk if I can't even talk her out of it." He sensed her worry. "Eliza, it's going to be okay, you know."

"I know," she said, confidently. "Thank you, Dmitrije."

"Don't thank me yet," he said, gathering his paper. "There are still a few bumps in the road ahead. I suspect you'll be cursing me before long when you start missing long days in the sun."

"Oh right," she scoffed, "that's so me."

He continued, "Or when you break something valuable because you lost your composure, or grow bored from having too much of it."

"All I'll need to do is talk to you," she shot back. "That should cure me of that."

He laughed. "It'll require at least three attempts to reach you before you pick up. But you will...eventually. And I'll walk you through whatever it is that's got you hating me. Before long, it will be me who needs walking through."

He threw a few dollars on the bill and slid out.

Eliza grabbed her money and followed him.

Eliza opened the door to room 718 and walked in. She grabbed her bags and was pleased at how light they felt. She stood there for a minute, holding them, and looked in the mirror. In her head she said goodbye to the broken little doll she was leaving behind. She knew that an imprint of her still existed somewhere under the new coat of paint, but she couldn't help but think that over time she would disappear entirely – lost, perhaps, in the mud behind a trailer in whatever little punch line town she belonged. If so, at least she said goodbye.

Dmitrije escorted Eliza to her car, holding a black umbrella above both of their heads. Without putting it down, he helped her put her bags into the back seat and closed the door. Then he folded it, and handed it to her.

"Take it," he insisted gently. "You'll be fine for a few hours in the car but we've only got a few minutes out here before we both start feeling faint. Comes with the territory, I'm afraid."

She took it from him and threw it into the front seat.

"I would say something touching and sentimental right now," she announced quietly, "but I don't do that kind of thing at the moment."

Dmitrije put his arms around her and pulled her in close.

"You will," he whispered. "You'll laugh and sing and cry... you'll even hurt like you want to die but it will pass. There will be longing and fear and loathing and even love, Eliza. Lots of love." He pulled away and looked in her eyes. "You showed me that."

"I did?" she said, noticing a tear running down his face.

"Yes...you. Thank *you*, Eliza Lowell." He touched her face, and placed a small kiss where his fingers had been. "Drive carefully, now."

He watched as she climbed into the car and closed the door behind her.

Eliza rolled down the window. "I forgot to ask," she cooed confidently. "What about sex? Will I still want it?"

Dmitrije snickered, and began walking away. Then he turned his head back to face her, using his hand to shield his eyes.

"Oh, yes," he said loudly, "it comes next after anger." With a wink, he turned his head back around and continued walking towards the hotel.

Eliza thought about that and, satisfied with his answer, started the car and backed out of the spot. Lily and Jesse flashed into her mind as she applied the brakes and shifted into first gear. By the time she was in second gear, she thought about running into the boys with the scraped fists at some point when she was home. If she did, she would have a few questions for them.

Then, with a punch of the gas she steered into the exit drive and maneuvered into the service road traffic.

As she headed for the main highway, she wondered if in six months she would remember the dozen or so pills that she had tossed into the mulch beneath the bushes, where the forces of time and rain would eventually dissolve them along with the hundreds of white cigarette butts.

Horror folks sure do like to smoke.

Eliza Lowell was a gypsy. Well, her ancestors were. That's what she chose to believe, anyway, as she pulled onto the highway and accelerated into the flow of traffic.

Dr. Dmitrije Radan knocked on the door, just under the numbers that read 537. It was his third time doing so. There was loud music coming from inside, so he was concerned that he may have to do it again. While he waited, he reached into his outside coat pocket and pulled out the two vampire teeth he had used as a prop to get Eliza's attention. He chuckled a little before putting them back. She must have done it when he was putting her bags into the car, or perhaps when he hugged her. A token of thanks, he assumed.

He had considered starting a vampire series – one more sympathetic to the species – if only to aid in his own cause. Now, maybe he had another reason: a young and beautiful one. Vampires were powerful, mythological constructs. They had been around for hundreds of years and were easy for the subconscious mind to grasp. The body, he learned, was accustomed to being ordered around by the brain. It was capable of so much if told the right things: like how to use one's pain in order to become something new, something strong yet sensitive to the pain of others, something resistant to the forces of physical change that made us old, weak, and vulnerable. Choosing to be a vampire (with a few minor alterations) meant he had a lineage, a crest of sorts – a family. He knew he was creative enough to build a mythological creature of his own that might have made it easier in some ways, but the vampire was there, waiting, as they do. Once you invited them in, all it took was a little convincing.

Finally the music was lowering, and someone was stomping towards the door. After the predictable pause at the peephole, he heard the chain coming off and took a half step back as the door opened.

"Hey, Doc!" said Francis, shouting a bit. His hair was wet and he had a towel around his neck. "Come on in."

Dmitrije entered and shut the door behind him.

"I hope you weren't out there long," Francis said apologetically. "I was in the shower and I had the music up."

Dmitrije knew exactly what had happened but it was nice, if highly unnecessary, of him to explain. In fact, it was fairly silly. He wouldn't go as far as to say it was stupid, but if he did he wouldn't be too far off the mark.

"I totally appreciate this, by the way. I'm, like, totally broke." He was talking as he searched for clothes among the wrinkled pile on the bed. "I blew everything at the bar, but fuck it. It was worth it."

Dmitrije reached into his pocket, pulled out the money clip, and slipped out a pair of twenties. "It's not a problem, Francis," he said, placing the bills on the desk in front of the mirror. "Like I told you on the phone, you saved me the trip."

Francis found the shirt he was looking for and said, "And she's not going to know about you paying me, right? I mean, it's not a huge deal or anything, but I really would have carried her stuff to the car for nothing."

"As agreed," replied Dmitrije.

"Awesome."

Francis pulled the towel from his neck and floated it over to the other side of the room. As he reversed his chosen shirt right side out, the skull tattoo on his chest – the one with the snakes crawling through the eyes – seemed to laugh with the jiggling of his fat. He looked up and saw Dmitrije looking at it.

"Yeah, you like it?" he bragged. "I got it at the last convention. I was pretty drunk and it's kind of shitty, but hey…you live and you learn, right?"

Dmitrije watched him pull on his shirt. As it draped over his eyes, it gave the former hypnotherapist just enough time to close the space between them. Once the shirt had gotten past his head and fallen around his neck, Francis had but a second to see him standing there before he was asleep.

Dmitrije steadied the portly predator with one hand and reached into his jacket pocket with the other. With a magician's flair, he withdrew several large syringes and pulled the cap off of one them with his teeth. He wasn't sure exactly how much he would take, but there was no doubt there would be enough for both he and Eliza to last until at least the next convention.

Scott Norton lives and writes at the New Jersey Shore where they roll up the sidewalks in winter. He also composes and performs "high energy modern rock" with a band called Surrounded by Idiots. For more info on his other novels and screenplays, check out www.scottStories.com.

www.ingramcontent.com/pod-product-compliance
Lightning Source LLC
Chambersburg PA
CBHW050825180626
46814CB00004B/1463
9780615239002